Death at the Drunken Duck

Veronica Vale Investigates - book 2

Kitty Kildare

K.E. O'Connor Books

Chapter 1

Why didn't every woman dream of standing in a muddy field surrounded by dogs, the wind blowing in her hair, and the sound of excited yips all around her? It was my idea of a perfect day. Fresh air, dogs, and plenty of exercise. It was just a pity I was surrounded by so many people.

I gently patted Benji's furry head as we took a break from the fun and games at the dogs' home outdoor charity event. The surprisingly sunny weather had brought out double the number of people we'd expected, and we were struggling to keep everything contained.

The dogs' home volunteers and the tiny number of paid staff were doing their best, but the air was tinged with chaos due to the presence of so many people, many of whom brought their own furry companions, and a number of well-mannered dogs from the home were on display. One wrong bark, and we could be in trouble.

"Do excuse me. Coming through, lady with a Pekinese. Mind your step, sir. Lady with tiny dog passing and she needs room to breathe." Ruby Smythe's determined voice carried through the crowd, although it took me a few seconds to locate her as she dodged past children munching on toffee apples and gossiping women strolling past the second-hand stores and tombola, looking for a bargain or hopeful of winning a bottle of sweet sherry when their ticket came up.

"Veronica! I thought I'd lost you." Ruby joined me, an adorable long-haired fluffy Pekinese snuggled against her. "Golly! It's hectic. I've had my foot trodden on twice."

I peered at her less than practical pale blue shoes that were splattered with mud, one of which had a clear imprint of a boot on it. "We'll get inside the show ring soon. It'll be less hectic away from the visitors."

She smiled as she gently dissuaded the Pekinese from licking her chin. "I just came from the volunteer stand. They've had over twenty applications to adopt the dogs we brought today. Isn't that marvellous!"

My heart fluttered with delight. That's what today was all about. We wanted everyone to see how amazing the dogs were and give them their forever homes. There was no space to take any new strays off the London streets, and we were desperate to get some pens empty so we could bring in the neediest of cases.

A red-faced man with a flat cap almost staggered into us, and only a warning growl from Benji, my delightful rescue dog, prevented a last-minute collision. The man tipped his cap at us, spilling ale from the tin cup he held as he mumbled his apology.

"Our rescue dogs are easy compared to these misbehaving people," I murmured.

Ruby laughed, never happier than when she was in the middle of fun. "I saw your uncle Harry a few minutes ago.

This is beneath him, though, isn't it? Covering a charity event for the newspaper. He's usually chasing leads on corrupt politicians."

"Uncle Harry is having a rare afternoon off," I said. "It took some persuading to get him out of the office."

"He's with that crumpled-looking chap. The one who's always complaining about you."

I grimaced. "Bob. He's the reporter officially covering today's event. Although you should have heard him moan when he was given the task. He said it wasn't a story for a respectable journalist to cover, and what was the point in writing about unwanted dogs nobody cared about?"

"I hope you gave him what for," Ruby said.

"Naturally, we exchanged heated words over the importance of the charity and how every home was better with a dog in it."

"Hah! What a delight that would have been to watch. He's got a face on him like a wet weekend," Ruby said. "I hope he writes a decent article."

"I'll make sure he does." Although my role at the London Times was limited to writing obituaries for the recently departed, I occasionally added my name to the byline of local interest pieces. And I'd be certain to check Bob's commentary on this event. The article needed to ensure the charity shone to maximise the chance of more dogs finding their perfect families.

"Let's head to the show ring," I said. "Get the dogs ready so everybody falls in love with them."

"I know I always say I don't have space in my life for a dog." Ruby followed me through the crowd as we artfully dodged people, the air alive with chatter and laughter. "But this little lady has won my heart."

I glanced over my shoulder. The Pekinese was fast asleep. "You're thinking of adopting her?"

"Oh, I don't know. Dogs are such a responsibility, and Lady M often makes me work late. Would it be fair to the dog? She'd be alone a lot."

"You could take her to work," I said. "So long as you're careful around the horses, I don't see it being a problem."

"She is sweet. I'll think about it. How about you? Have you seen any dogs that have captured your heart?"

Every dog I met captured my heart, but I didn't have room for all of them. "I'm content with Benji." I paused as a group of children dashed past, their faces smeared with chocolate and their eyes alive with happiness.

"I suppose you want a break after handling that German Shepherd. I lost count of the number of times he knocked me over," Ruby said. "He had no manners!"

We continued our journey towards the roped-off patch of grass that would serve as our show ring. "He was a handful. But we found him a perfect home with that farmer. The Shepherd will make a perfect guard dog and is already getting along famously with the sheep. He was under-stimulated, living with me. And even Benji couldn't keep up with his antics."

Benji cocked an ear and wagged his tail, suggesting he knew what we spoke about. He was such a clever dog.

I'd temporarily fostered the German Shepherd after his owner died. In my position as an obituary writer, the local police had gotten to know I could be called upon when they discovered an animal in a deceased person's property. And with my connection to the dogs' home in

Battersea, I could be relied upon to find a place for the animals.

But this German Shepherd had needed special attention. He'd been poorly trained and had a tendency to use his teeth rather than think. It had taken many hours of training using his favourite squeaky ball before he'd learned the appropriate manners. But I never gave up on a dog. To my mind, there was no such thing as a bad dog, just a badly behaved owner.

Molly Banbury appeared beside us. "There you are, ladies. I need you in the show ring." She was the dogs' home's reliable receptionist, although she stretched her role far beyond those duties. She was a sprightly fifty with a mess of tight ginger curls and wore an eye patch, having sustained serious injuries during a bombing in the East End during the Great War.

"We're ready when you are," Ruby said.

"You can take another dog, Ruby, since that tiny Pekinese is no bother," Molly said. "Veronica, you're with the greyhound."

I nodded my agreement. I was happy to focus on my volunteering again. Life finally felt back to normal after the previous month's shock when we discovered the lifeless body of Florence Sterling, a prominent theatre star and friend of the family. After some investigation, I'd discovered, with the exquisite help of Ruby and Benji, Florence had been attacked in a pub owned by my family. Following significant delving and a number of heated debates with the police, who considered our assistance unwelcome, we uncovered the appropriate clues, and the police caught the criminals.

With that matter put to bed, I'd focused on my job at the newspaper, caring for my elderly mother, and devoting my remaining time to the dogs' home. They were my three great passions.

Molly cheerfully yelled out orders to other volunteers to collect the dogs and assemble in the show ring. The pinnacle of the day was a series of fun events the dogs would take part in. We had obedience, waggiest tail, fastest ball capture, and most handsome face. Of course, the dogs weren't forced to do anything. Some were a little skittish, which was why we were doing this showcase. Hopefully, there would be a perfect family watching the dogs parade around the show ring, and they'd fall in love and adopt them.

Molly marched over and handed me the lead of a large pale-furred greyhound. Her name was Bambi, although she rarely answered to that name. She was a free-spirited dog who liked one long walk a day and spent the rest of her time sleeping in her pen. She was a big, gangly dog with a long thin nose and dark liquid eyes. A real beauty.

Half a dozen of the dog show volunteers lined up, each with two dogs. Ruby still carried her Pekinese, but also held the lead of an adorable high-spirited Jack Russell with a white heart splodge on his side.

Molly grabbed a loudspeaker, making it squeal to get people's attention. "Roll up, roll up, everybody. It's time for the most magnificent part of today. Give a warm, quiet welcome to our amazing dogs available for adoption. Don't be shy about meeting them afterwards. They're ready for a new home, and they're excited to meet you. If you want to learn more about any of the dogs, visit the volunteer stand at the side of the show ring, and we'll tell you all about them."

And then we were off! We'd planned to walk three circuits of the ring, then take the dogs back to their pens where they'd be safely and comfortably secured before it became too overwhelming.

Bambi started with enthusiastic, chaotic vigour. She was keen on playing with Benji, who was on his best behaviour as he walked beside me and not in the mood to play when he knew he should set an example for the other dogs.

I fished a piece of sausage from my jacket pocket and encouraged Bambi to walk beside me, keeping the treat pinched between my fingers so she'd have to fight to get it. She achieved focus for three seconds before leaping up and down several times.

My eyebrows lifted as I spotted Inspector Jacob Templeton standing with another police officer close to the ropes. "Good afternoon, Inspector! Finally ready to adopt that dog, are you?"

He held up a hand. "Just passing through. Your one looks a handful."

"Bambi is adorable. You should meet her afterwards."

He shook his head, his dark eyes warm with amusement as he watched me fail to get Bambi under control.

By the time we were on our final circuit, I was down to my last few pieces of sausage and hoped I'd have enough to keep Bambi settled. She was an adorable dog, but had a stronger will than me.

Uncle Harry waved at me from the crowd, his white shirt unbuttoned at the collar, his tie flipped over one shoulder. "We've got great photographs. Bob will write an amazing article to go with them."

Bob slouched beside Uncle Harry, looking like this was the last place he wanted to be.

"So long as we do the dogs proud, that's all I care about," I called out. The flash of a camera bulb temporarily dazzled me. It wasn't our newspaper's general assistant, Ernie Clipper, taking the picture, and I was less than pleased to discover Isabella Michaels, holding aloft her camera, a thin smile on her face.

Isabella worked for a rival newspaper in London, a tattle sheet that spread gossip to titillate the public. She arched a brow, her grin sharp. "The mud-splattered look suits you. And Ruby Smythe! You look like a common farmer's wife."

"There's nothing common about me. And I've met many farmers I'd be more than happy to date." Ruby lifted her chin as the Pekinese attempted to lick her face again. "Rather than being unkind, join in. This is a charity event, after all. I hope you've made a sizeable donation to this excellent cause."

"We're covering the event in the newspaper. That's my nod to charity," Isabella said. "Although I've yet to find any interesting stories. We may not bother to take it to print if the day remains so unstimulating."

Bambi jerked her lead, almost pulling me off my feet. She grabbed something out of the mud and gobbled it down. Before I could investigate what she'd picked up, something landed by my feet. It was a piece of sausage!

Bambi ate it, and her head shot up as she looked for more treats, her ears pricked.

"Is someone throwing food?" I glared at Isabella, but she was doing something to her camera. I looked around the crowd, and my gaze settled on Bob. He was smirking. Uncle Harry had his back to him as he chatted with someone in the throng.

I narrowed my eyes at Bob, then gently encouraged Bambi to continue her walk. We had half a lap to go, and I was certain she would make it with no more incidents. I'd only taken a few steps before more sausage missiles launched at me. Bambi couldn't contain herself. She barked in excitement and lurched forward. My feet slipped out from underneath me, and I landed face-first in the mud.

Isabella's laughter hit me a few seconds later, and as I rolled over, coating myself in muck, she was taking photographs. The very nerve of that woman.

"Now this is what I call a story," Isabella said. "Veronica Vale Eats Dirt!"

"Stop that greyhound!" I attempted to scramble to my feet, but they slipped from underneath me, and I landed on my backside this time with a pained grunt. That made Isabella laugh even more, and several members of the crowd joined in and started pointing.

I attempted to stand again, but landed heavily on my right hip, and it throbbed a warning not to move. But I couldn't stay in the mud. If I wasn't careful, I'd be jumped on by several overexcited dogs, especially if there was more of Bob's sausage lying around.

Benji sniffed my cheek and gently whined in my ear.

"No harm done. At least, nothing broken." I puffed out a breath and focused on getting up without making a fool of myself.

A shadow appeared over me, and I looked up. Inspector Templeton had his hand held out. "It looks like you could do with some assistance."

Chapter 2

By the time I'd gotten to my feet, ably assisted by Inspector Templeton, we were both mud splattered. He had a smear of mud on the sleeve of his shirt and a mud imprint from my hand where I'd grabbed his bicep as I'd slipped again.

"You went down hard that last time," Inspector Templeton said. "Anything damaged?"

"I bruised my hip, but I've had worse. Thank you for the help." My furious gaze went to Isabella, but she'd disappeared into the crowd. She was most likely going back to the newspaper to get the story written up, and the photographs developed. What a humiliation.

"What was that dog doing?" Inspector Templeton asked. "It got a burst of energy just before it tugged you over."

"That burst of energy was thanks to a hateful colleague, who thought hurling cooked meat at me would be entertaining. He knew how it would make the dog behave. What dog can resist a piece of sausage?" I grimaced at my filthy clothing and tugged down my crumpled jacket. "Now, I'd like you to arrest Mr Robert Flanders for me."

"Robert?"

"The sausage thrower! Bob!" I said. "The man is a menace and an idiot. And he assaulted me."

"With cooked sausage?" Inspector Templeton looked mildly perplexed. "I'm unsure if I can arrest someone for that. Where is he?"

I pointed to the spot Bob had been standing a moment ago, but just like Isabella, he'd skulked off. No doubt, he'd seen I was being assisted by a police officer and scarpered. Inspector Templeton was well known about these parts. "Bob doesn't approve of a woman working in the newspaper office. He thinks I should be chained to the kitchen sink with half a dozen children running around my feet. He delights in pointing out any failings I encounter, even if they're of his own making."

Before Inspector Templeton could pass comment, Ruby appeared.

"Veronica! I caught Bambi." She was accompanied by three dogs: the Pekinese, the friendly Jack Russell, and Bambi.

"Inspector Templeton, take this." She dumped the Pekinese into his arms. "She's well-behaved, and so light, you'll barely know you're holding her. And since you're already covered in mud, you won't mind a little fur, too."

Inspector Templeton stared down at the dog and shook his head.

"Take this one, as well." Ruby handed him the Jack Russell's lead. She kept a firm hold on Bambi. "I saw what happened. Goodness, you went down with a thump. It made the ground shake."

"It was because of Bob being his usual buffoon-like self," I said. "He brought cooked sausage here to ruin things. When I find him, I'll give him what for. And Inspector Templeton has agreed to arrest him."

"I never said that."

"Don't worry about Bob," Ruby said. "I saw your uncle Harry giving him an ear bashing on the other side of the show ring. He must have seen what he was up to. You didn't get injured, did you?"

"Veronica hurt her hip," Inspector Templeton said. "I was checking to see if there were any more injuries."

"Please, don't concern yourselves," I said. "I'm made of stern stuff, and I'm not afraid of a little mud."

"You can't be injured!" Ruby said. "It's Lady Sybil's party tonight."

"I'll be fine for the party. But I would like a sit down."

"You'd better be fine. There'll be dancing all evening."

"Lady Sybil?" Inspector Templeton asked.

"Lady Sybil Montague is holding a party at her home in Epsom," I said.

"I've been looking forward to the event for a long time," Ruby said. "I can't wait to get there and hear the latest gossip. I still can't believe Arthur is dating her."

"Arthur Braithwaite," I explained to Inspector Templeton. "Ruby and Arthur had a dalliance not so long ago."

"It was more than a dalliance! I was convinced that man intended to marry me. He made all the right noises about turning me into an honest woman. But when he realised, I'm almost as poor as a church mouse, he turned his attentions to Lady Sybil. She's disgustingly rich and attractive for a mature woman." Ruby feigned a dramatic sigh. "Once he'd set his sights on her, it was as if I'd never existed. Rich beats pretty every time."

"I am sorry to hear that." Inspector Templeton's tone suggested he had no clue how to respond to Ruby's flurry of information regarding her romantic entanglements.

"You were never serious with Arthur," I said soothingly. "Although he's a nice chap, he's unreliable. A bit of a cad, if you ask me. You don't want to become serious with a cad."

"He could be a touch roguish," Ruby said, "but he's handsome and as charming as they come. Almost as charming as you, Inspector. Don't you think, Veronica?"

"I really couldn't say." I busied myself by brushing at the mud on my jacket and smearing it down my thigh.

Ruby laughed and leaned closer to Inspector Templeton. "After I refused to speak to Arthur for months, we formed a truce. I value his friendship, and now he's involved with Lady Sybil, we get the opportunity to attend some incredible events. Although this will be the first time I've been to Lady Sybil's residence. She lives in a stunning mansion. Apparently, there are twenty bedrooms!"

"I'm aware of Lady Sybil Montague," Inspector Templeton said. "Her late husband worked in financing in the city, didn't he?"

"He did," I said. "How do you know that?"

"He was a friend of Detective Chief Inspector Taylor. They golfed together. And I remember Lord Montague attending a few policemen's benevolent events."

"Now Lady Sybil's a fabulously wealthy widow and is loving life," Ruby said. "She's certainly loving the attention she's getting from the younger men. More's the pity. I could be married by now if she wasn't so filthy rich."

"It was gracious of Arthur to invite us to the party," I said diplomatically.

"There was nothing gracious about it. I told him to," Ruby said. "It was compensation for how badly he treated me. You know Arthur, he's an easy-going chap and took no offence. It'll be a fun party. I even have a new dress."

"I'm sure you'll both look lovely." Inspector Templeton's gaze lingered on me.

"Let's finish here, and then we can relax and have a nice cup of tea before we get ready for the evening's excitement," I said.

"Nice cup of tea? I intend to have a dry martini," Ruby said. "Inspector Templeton, perhaps we could secure you an invitation to the party? Do you like to dance?"

"Thank you, but I must decline," he said.

"How about you adopt a dog, then?" I asked.

He shook his head. "I'm simply here to ensure order is maintained."

"What about the Jack Russell?" I inclined my head at the perky-looking chap sitting by Inspector Templeton's feet. "He likes you."

"He'll be someone's perfect dog, but he's not mine." Inspector Templeton handed the lead to Ruby. "I'm glad you weren't badly hurt when you took a tumble, Veronica. Enjoy the rest of your day." He turned and walked away.

"How heroic of him to come to your rescue," Ruby said. "I saw the whole thing. He leaped the rope and ran to assist you."

"Then you may need glasses, because it was barely a rescue," I said tartly. "I fell, and he helped me up."

"You were free enough with your hands when he helped," Ruby said. "You grabbed his arm!"

My cheeks grew warm. He had delectable arms. "This patch of ground is remarkably slippery, and I lost my footing several times. What else should I have grabbed to stop myself from falling again?"

Ruby chuckled. "Inspector Templeton wasn't offended. Any man would be happy to be grabbed by you. And that particular man is sweet on you."

"Let's see how much money the event has made so far, shall we?" I was not having this conversation with Ruby again. My heart was closed to romance. It had been rudely trodden on by a man I'd trusted, and I had no desire or inclination to repeat that unfortunate episode ever again.

We spent the next two hours in a whirlwind of activity, attending the different dog shows, and helping with enquiries about the dogs available for adoption. At the end of the event, all but two of the dogs had adoption forms filled in, we'd raised ten pounds for the dogs' home, and I'd developed a throb in my right hip and a limp, which I was doing my best to hide from Ruby.

"Ready to go?" Ruby discovered me after I'd snuck into a small marquee and found a chair to rest on. "Gosh! You look unwell. You're terribly pale."

"It's been a busy day," I said. "Although I'm happy Benji won the most obedient dog award. He's such a good boy."

Benji proudly sat beside me with a small red rosette pinned to his collar.

Ruby grabbed a wooden chair and joined us. "You need to catch your second wind before tonight's party. I can't decide whether to wear my new blue sleeveless dress with the beads, or my faithful cream. It never lets me down."

"You'll look stunning whatever you wear," I said. "All heads will turn when you walk into the room."

"Tosh and nonsense. They will look at you," Ruby said. "Although brush the mud out of your hair."

"It's a beauty treatment. I read about it in a magazine." I picked a chunk of dried mud from my hair.

Ruby laughed. "Then we'll both be belles of the ball. Hurry! We can collect my things, and I'll change at your house. Then we'll drive over together."

I resisted the urge to groan as I stood, my throbbing hip telling me the best thing to do would be to take a hot bath and then lie down in a dark room and sleep. But I'd soldier on. There were several friends attending the party, and it had been an age since I'd spent time with Ruby's family. It was just her younger brother Todd Smythe who'd be attending, but he was great fun.

After saying goodbye and thanking the volunteers from the dogs' home, I plodded to Ruby's sizeable Ghost with Benji, settled in, and we drove to my family home, close to Seven Sister's Road in Finsbury Park. I had my own room and an indoor bathroom, and my mother took a mere trifle for the rent, and only when I pressed it upon her. We also had space for unexpected guests. The human and animal kind. My brother Matthew was currently looking after a bundle of sweet kittens.

Once Ruby was parked, we headed inside, careful to take off mud-splattered shoes and coats to avoid treading dirt through the house.

My mother, Edith Vale, called out a greeting from her bed in the downstairs front parlour she'd commandeered.

I poked my head into the room. "Everything good?"

"It's dreadful. I've had no company all day. I didn't know you'd be out this long." My mother had grey-white hair and lines around her mouth that always made her look like she was frowning. But despite the stern exterior, she had a soft heart and a love of animals almost as big as mine.

"Didn't Sally pop by for a cup of tea?" I asked. "She said she would."

"Oh, just her. And Mrs Parker from number ten came by for a couple of hours. That woman can talk the hind legs off a donkey."

"And hasn't Matthew been here all day?" My younger brother preferred to stay indoors.

"Of course. The boy never goes out."

"So ... you haven't been alone all day?"

Mother sighed. "You've not been here. How was the dog show?"

"Benji won a rosette for being the most obedient dog."

Benji trotted into my mother's bedroom and rested his head on the edge of the bed so she could pat him, and he could show off his rosette.

"He's such a good boy. So much better than the German Shepherd. I'm sure an unnatural spirit possessed that creature," my mother said.

"He just needed the right home. He's loving life on the farm. And I know you secretly miss him." Although my mother complained every time I brought a new foster animal home, she adored the company and was always sad when they left.

Ruby glided in, having been in the kitchen getting the water boiled for tea. "Edith, come to the party with us. Get out of that bed and enjoy a dance." She kissed my mother's cheek.

"Foolish girl. I can barely stand. Dancing a jig would do me in."

"You'd have a marvellous time. And Lady Sybil will have the best champagne." Ruby held out the dresses she'd brought with her. "Which one should I choose tonight? The blue or the cream?"

"The blue," my mother said. "Although the cream is lovely."

As they discussed dresses, I eased into a chair in the corner of my mother's room and stretched out my leg.

"Veronica!"

My head jerked up. "Sorry, it's been a busy day."

"You must be unwell," my mother said, concern showing in her eyes. "You've barely uttered a word since you came home."

I looked around the room. "Where's Ruby?"

"Gone to freshen the tea. What's the matter with you? Did you inhale London smog? It's treacherous stuff."

"No smog! But I am tired." I leaned forward. "Don't tell Ruby, but I'd rather have an early night than go to this party."

"I heard that! Get this drink down you, and you'll change your mind." Ruby sailed into the room carrying a laden tea tray. There was a pot of tea, cups, and three large glasses of brandy.

"Oh, I really shouldn't drink, not with my heart the way it is." My mother eagerly swept a brandy glass off the tray and sipped it.

"You'll feel more cheerful when you're in a fancy frock and I've made you up with my latest lipstick." Ruby pushed a glass of brandy into my hand. "Drink up. This will warm you from the inside out."

I muttered a weary thank you. The brandy would perk me up, and I was sure once I was at the party, I'd enjoy myself. But sitting in my mother's overly warm room in a comfortable chair, I could think of nowhere else I wanted to be.

"Arthur said there'll be several single men at the party." Ruby dashed in and out of the room, in her different dresses, seeking input from my mother, then changing her mind about which one she preferred.

"I'm sure they'll be delightful company," I said.

"It is time you found yourself a nice young man," my mother said. "After all that business with—"

"We don't talk about him," I said. "That business is in the past, where it needs to stay."

Ruby dashed back in wearing the blue dress. She settled her hands on her hips. "The problem is, it's clearly not in your past, since you're not looking at any other man. Well, there is Inspector Templeton. He's dashing. Even though you covered him in mud today, he still looked handsome."

"What's this?" my mother asked. "What did you do to poor Inspector Templeton?"

I groaned. "Nothing. Ruby, dress me and cover me in makeup. Then let's find you an unsuitable man at this party."

Chapter 3

"Is everything quite right with you?" Ruby enquired as she sped along the increasingly narrow country lanes towards Kempton Park. "You've been shifting around in your seat as if you have a feather in your undergarments."

"I'm stiff after today's adventures." In truth, my hip troubled me. Despite finishing the brandy and putting my best foot forward, I felt less than sprightly.

"You're as fit as a flea," Ruby said. "A quick trot around the muddy showground shouldn't have tired you. Maybe your mother is right, and you're coming down with something. Do you feel cold or clammy?"

"It's nothing. I'll be fine once we get to the party." I winced as Ruby hit a bump in the road and gripped the edge of my seat. Ruby was a proficient driver but enjoyed pushing the Ghost to its limits. The car had been a gift from a former admirer, and after they'd separated, Ruby had kept it. The poor chap had no option but to oblige her since he was due overseas the following month and felt more than a trifle guilty for being seen out with another woman while courting Ruby.

"I'm so excited to catch up with Todd," Ruby said. "I haven't seen him in over a month."

"He's always excellent fun. It's a shame the rest of your family couldn't attend the gathering."

"Duke is still out of the country." Ruby waggled her eyebrows. "I'm sure you'll miss his fond attentions."

I shook my head, a rueful smile on my face. Duke Smythe was the world's most extravagant flirt. He was so good at flirting that he'd almost convinced me I was his one and only, before Ruby put me in my place and informed me he flirted with all the pretty faces. I didn't hold it against him. Duke was a splendid party companion, and whenever you were in his presence, you could be guaranteed a good time.

"Any news on Lily?" I asked.

Ruby pulled a face. "That haughty madam would consider she was slumming it to come to a gathering in such a small mansion."

"She's not that bad," I gently chided.

"Ever since she married into the Columbus family, she's been a nightmare. All I hear about is the expensive silverware and the china she's collecting. Honestly, when she comes back to this country, it'll cost a small fortune to have it all shipped over. Perhaps she has no plans to come home ever again. She has abandoned her poor relatives now she's struck gold with a rich husband. Lucky thing."

I smiled as Ruby berated her younger sister's good fortune at landing a wealthy Italian husband who'd made his money in the oil industry. Not the crude oil industry, but rather, olive oil. He had acres of land covered in olive trees and sold premium products across Europe.

"We'll have plenty of fun with Todd and his friends," I said. "And I'd like to see how he's getting on with Pippin."

"Oh, you have nothing to worry about there." Ruby took a bend on the racing line. "He adores Pippin. He keeps buying her things, even though he can ill afford to."

"They seem to be getting on so well." Several weeks ago, Todd had stopped by the dogs' home, seeking a furry companion. We'd matched him with an adorable mutt called Pippin, who was only two years old. They'd hit it off, and I was thrilled to give Pippin such a welcoming home.

Ruby inched her foot off the accelerator and squinted over the car's bonnet. "Any second now, there should be the turning that'll take us to Lady Sybil's house. It's a private driveway. Watch out for it."

"If you slowed to an acceptable pace, we'd see it more easily, and you'd not have to execute a dangerous manoeuvre at the last—"

"There it is!" Ruby took a sharp left, causing the tires to protest, and Benji to yip his surprise as he rolled on the back seat.

The route took us along the driveway towards Lady Sybil's house. Gravel crunched under the car's tires as we passed neatly manicured bushes and a tidy expanse of lawn. The Ghost's headlights slowly illuminated the mansion. An exquisite pale stone building with columns on either side of the grand front entrance, which was lit up from the inside. Every room had lights on. There were two enormous chimney stacks at either end of the roof and stone steps leading up to the front door.

"Oh, my goodness." Ruby stamped on the brake and stared at the house. "When Arthur said Lady Sybil was worth a few bob, he wasn't joking."

"I looked her up in the newspaper archives," I said. "When her husband died, he left Lady Sybil everything. Several houses, his business, which she sold for a fortune, and apparently, there were assets abroad. She is set for several lifetimes."

"Todd told me she's been holding parties every month, so it would appear she's happy to spend that fortune. Still, why shouldn't she have fun? Maybe her late husband was a horror and held the purse strings tightly. Now he's gone, Lady Sybil is letting her hair down, and we're reaping the benefits."

I let Benji out of the back of the car so he could stretch and sniff before we went inside. I'd put a bright red neckerchief on him, and he looked even more handsome than ever. It matched my pretty fringed shawl, which Ruby insisted I bring because my dress was black and considered dour. Her words, not mine.

While Benji sniffed, we stood in the cool evening air, examining the house's grandeur. Out of the open windows, laughter drifted, and I could hear lively music.

"It's already in full swing," Ruby said. "Todd said Lady Sybil's been hosting all week. Special guests of the family, I believe. Most likely a few friends of Arthur's, too."

"Let's get inside and see what's going on." I walked with a barely noticeable limp, and we climbed the stone steps. Before we reached the door, it was opened by a tidily attired butler, who greeted us, checked our names off the guest list, and then took our coats and purses.

The inside of the house was no less grand than the outside. A majestic hallway stretched before us, adorned with intricately patterned Art déco wallpaper, and the crystal chandeliers overhead cast a warm, golden glow, reflecting off the polished marble floors. Antique Persian rugs sprawled underfoot, adding a touch of richness to the already sumptuous surroundings.

Oil paintings adorned the walls, depicting scenes of the English countryside, as a nod to the mansion's heritage and a reminder of the timeless beauty of the Surrey landscape.

"There you are!" Todd Smythe bounded over, his dark hair longer than the current fashion, and dropping into his sparkling brown eyes. He was twenty-eight, two years younger than Ruby, and always dressed in the latest style. Tonight, it was a dashing dark suit with silk facings and a crisp white shirt.

He hugged Ruby tightly, then stepped back and kissed my cheek.

Ruby whacked him on the arm. "Are we late? You told us to be here at eight o'clock."

"Your timing is perfect," Todd said with a chuckle. "Lady Sybil has had people here all day. They had an early dinner and got things going before the rest of the guests arrived."

"You were here for dinner?" I asked.

Todd nodded. "Arthur invited me along so I could meet a few new people. The food was excellent." He patted his stomach. "Let me introduce you to Lady Sybil. This way!"

Todd dashed off, leaving us with no option but to hurry after him. He approached a short, plump woman dressed in a swathe of expensive silk, diamonds on her earlobes, and a tiara in her dark hair. She looked like royalty. She turned away from the person she was speaking to and smiled at Todd.

"Lady Sybil, I'd like you to meet my sister, Ruby, and her best friend, Veronica Vale. And this is Benji."

Lady Sybil's light brown eyes skimmed over us. They hardened for a second when she saw Benji, but she made no comment about him attending the party without a formal invitation. "Welcome to my little gathering."

"Thank you for having us. Is the party for any particular reason?" Ruby asked. "We were so thrilled to get an invitation, but I didn't know if it was your birthday or an anniversary."

"No special reason. Why can't one have a party simply for the sake of having a party?" Lady Sybil asked, her voice low for a woman, and husky, suggesting she was a regular smoker.

"Spot on! I absolutely adore a party," Ruby said.

"When I told your brother what I had planned, he was excited to invite you. Of course, being such a close friend with Arthur, I could hardly refuse him. It's always nice to make new friends, don't you think?"

"We're looking forward to this evening," I said.

"Todd, be a dear and fetch drinks for everyone," Lady Sybil said. "And take Miss Vale's dog outside."

"He stays with me," I said firmly. "Benji is well-behaved. I'll ensure he doesn't wander and bother everyone. He doesn't like to be left alone, though."

Lady Sybil pursed her lips a fraction. "I can't understand everyone's fascination with dogs. Todd, where is yours? Not being a pest again, is it?"

"Pippin is around. The last time I saw her, she was begging food off a pretty lady in a gold dress."

"I don't want it bothering my guests. Put the dog on a lead if you have to. Or better yet, let it outside. We have empty stables."

"I know Pippin," I said. "She won't do well in a cold, dark stable on her own. Rescue animals need careful handling."

"I can't say I know anything about that." Lady Sybil gently pressed the diamonds in her ear. "Very well. The creatures may stay. But if anyone complains, I want them gone. Todd, where are those drinks?"

"I'm getting them now." Todd bounded away, an always moving ball of happiness and energy.

Lady Sybil turned to us. "Enjoy your evening. If you'll excuse me, I have other guests to attend to."

Ruby caught hold of my elbow the second Lady Sybil drifted away. "Not the warmest of welcomes."

"Perhaps not," I said. "And she doesn't like dogs."

"Never a good character trait," Ruby said. "If Lady Sybil has anything against horses, we won't be friendly."

I smiled at my horse-mad friend. "I couldn't agree more."

Todd returned a moment later with glasses of champagne for us to raise a toast to the party and then led us into a grand parlour full of people. "Let me introduce you to some of my friends. Arthur, get over here!" He gestured wildly to a dapper-looking chap in a well-tailored grey suit with a white waistcoat who leaned rather too close to a serving maid. Arthur swayed slightly on his feet as he came towards us, but his smile was warm and made his handsome features even more appealing.

"Arthur Buchanan, you know my sister, Ruby, and this is her best friend, Veronica Vale. Have you met, before?"

"I feel like we have, but Ruby never introduced us." We exchanged a few pleasantries while sipping on champagne.

"Good thing too," Ruby said, tearing her gaze from the dancing. "Arthur would only have flirted with you and embarrassed himself."

Arthur tugged at his collar. "Steady on, old girl. I'm a happily settled man these days."

Ruby gently snorted.

"I'm glad there are more people here my own age," Arthur said. "We had to separate the oldies from everyone else because they weren't happy about all the racket."

"There are two separate parties going on?" I enquired.

"Most of them have gone home," Arthur said. "But they were complaining about us youngsters being noisy. They're Lady Sybil's lot from the tennis club. Boring old things, but you didn't hear me say that."

"It's a party. Noise is to be expected," Ruby said.

"Lady Sybil likes to include everyone at her parties," Arthur explained. "She's got such a generous nature. That's why I'm so fond of her. Although that old bunch just wanted to swap war stories."

"And we have none to share." Todd tapped Arthur's chest. "We have the same condition."

"I never thought I'd be more grateful to have a dicky ticker." Arthur chortled, along with Todd.

I studied Arthur while he chatted with Ruby and Todd about the party and pointed out various people of note. There was perhaps ten to twelve years' difference in age between Arthur and Lady Sybil. Considering the shortage of eligible bachelors available since the Great War ended, I was surprised he'd formed a relationship with an older woman. Could the grand surroundings and endless parties be the reason he was so fond of her?

"If you'd like to join us later, I'm putting together a card game," Arthur said. "Just a small wager, mainly for fun."

"I'm dreadful at cards," Ruby said. "Apparently, I have the worst poker face."

"Too right! You squeak every time you get a good hand," Todd said.

That comment earned him another thump.

"I do not squeak. Take that back."

"There'll be no gambling tonight." A dour-faced woman in her early thirties appeared beside us, dressed in an unglamourous tweed suit, her dark hair pulled back in a severe bun and a scowl on her face.

"Steady on, Emma," Arthur said. "It's just for laughs. Join us. You never know, you may enjoy yourself."

"Gambling should be illegal, no matter what you're using as the stakes. And you should know better than to persuade others to get involved in your foolishness. It only leads to trouble."

"Don't mind my sister. She was born grumpy," Arthur said, although he squeezed Emma's arm as he spoke. "This is Emma Wainwright."

My attention drifted to the small fluffy dog Emma had settled on one hip. The softness of the fur indicated it was well looked after.

"Is that a pedigree?" I asked.

"She is. Why the interest?" Emma peered down her nose at me.

"I'm connected to the dogs' home in Battersea," I said. "Veronica Vale."

"I know the place. I've even been by a few times with donations."

"Did you get your dog from the shelter? I don't remember seeing her available for adoption."

"No, she's not a rescue. I've had her since she was a pup." Emma's expression softened.

Arthur went to pet the dog, but she snapped her tiny teeth at him. He drew back his hand and cursed. "Damned creature."

"You startled her. Poor baby." Emma turned and stomped away, talking to the dog and glaring at any party goer who got too close.

"The creature is a menace." Arthur inspected his fingers. "Her personality is almost as dour as my sister's. It's why they get along so well."

Ruby let out a startled yelp and hopped into the air. An older red-cheeked man in a wheelchair had run into her.

"My dear, a thousand apologies," he said. "Although, I'm almost not sorry since I've seen how pretty your face is. I hope I didn't injure your lovely legs. Would you like me to look for any bruises?"

Ruby rubbed her ankle. "No harm done. Do you need a hand getting around? It's crowded in here."

"Let me help, John." Arthur grabbed the back of the chair. He leaned in close to the group. "Watch out. John likes a drink, and when that happens, he loses control of his wheels and the ability to keep his hands to himself.

I'll park him somewhere with a large scotch and be right back."

When Arthur returned, another man accompanied him. Similar age, almost as handsome, although he had striking pale blond hair and a gap between his front teeth.

"Ladies, I must introduce you to Peter Appleby. One of my closest friends and an all-round good egg."

Peter grinned warmly and nodded at us as introductions were made. "Now we can have fun. Would you ladies like to dance?"

Chapter 4

Two hours of dancing in an overly warm, crowded room, full of noise, laughter, and cigarette smoke, and I was worn out. Not only did my hip throb, but my feet also joined in the protest. Ruby had convinced me to wear less-than-practical shoes, and I deeply regretted it. Add to that the headache that had been growing for fifteen minutes, and I knew it was time to leave this party.

I excused myself from dancing with Todd and edged out of the room. I'd lost sight of Ruby a short time ago as she'd gone to get drinks with Peter. They'd hit it off and barely left each other's side. They were dancing together, laughing together, or whispering to each other. I'd keep an eye on that relationship. Ruby fell in love with the snap of a caddish finger but had gotten her heart broken numerous times by untrustworthy types who promised her the world but vanished before delivering the dreams they sold her.

I heard Ruby's familiar laugh, slightly louder than usual, most likely due to the champagne, and I followed the sound. I collected Benji en route as he'd waited patiently in a quiet room away from the guests with several other dogs, including the adorable Pippin.

I discovered Ruby standing too close to be respectable to Peter as they joked about something.

She looked up as I approached. "Having fun?"

"Too much fun. I'm calling it a night."

"Oh! Are you sure?" Ruby frowned. "Apparently, Lady Sybil's parties can go on until dawn."

I failed to hide my grimace. "It's been such a long day that I need an early night."

Ruby looked at Peter, and her bottom lip jutted out. "I'll come with you."

I sighed. "Stay if you're having fun."

"That's an excellent idea," Peter said brightly. "I'll look after Ruby."

"No, I should go with Veronica," Ruby said, with no small degree of reluctance. "I drove us here."

"If you trust me with the Ghost on the country lanes, I'm happy to get myself home." It wouldn't be the first time I'd driven Ruby's car, and I could handle such a vehicle without concern.

"You own a Rolls Royce?" Peter asked. "That's my favourite car."

Ruby twinkled under Peter's excitement. "We can take a look before Veronica leaves." She retrieved her purse from the butler, then handed me the key to unlock the Ghost. "Take great care of her. Are you sure you don't want me to drive?"

I leaned in close. "Enjoy yourself. But be careful not to have too much fun."

She looked at me with wide, amused eyes. "I'm always careful. Come along, Peter. We'll wave Veronica off, and you can inspect my glorious vehicle."

"I'm taking a turn around the garden to cool off before I go, so have fun inspecting the car. I'll see you tomorrow and you can let me know what I missed."

"Have no fear for Ruby's safety," Peter said. "I'll make sure she gets home."

I didn't find his charm convincing, and I detected the smell of whiskey on his breath. "Perhaps Todd should drive you."

Ruby laughed. "I don't trust that ninny behind the wheel. I wouldn't even trust him on a bicycle. He's so accident prone. I'll figure something out. Maybe Lady Sybil will find me a spare room if I get stuck."

"I'm staying overnight, too," Peter said. "There are plenty of bedrooms to choose from. Perhaps I could show you mine."

"You should stay at the party," I said firmly. "You don't want rumours spreading about what you two have been up to, do you?"

Peter's cheeks flushed. "Of course. Quite right."

Ruby glared at me as she tucked her arm into Peter's elbow. "Let's go."

I watched them leave and let out a soft sigh. Peter was full of fun, but I had a feeling he didn't take life seriously. Though Ruby could be a little too flippant, so perhaps they were a perfect match.

"Want a walk, boy?" I said to Benji, who had waited patiently beside me.

He wagged his tail at the sound of one of his favourite words, and ambled next to me as we exited the noise. I looked around to thank Lady Sybil for an enjoyable evening, but she was nowhere to be found.

I discovered a side gate that led into a quiet garden and walked along the dark path. It was cool and quiet, exactly what I needed after the heat and buzz of the inside. Inhaling lungfuls of fresh air, my headache eased. I enjoyed a party, but always welcomed my bed. I was never happier than when I rose early to achieve the day's tasks and didn't miss the morning.

Still, the gathering had been amusing. Todd was in high spirits, entertaining everyone, and when Arthur hadn't been running around after Lady Sybil, he'd been fun, too. As had Ruby's new friend, Peter. All in all, it was a successful event.

Raised voices reached me, and I slowed on the path. It was two male voices, and neither sounded happy. One sounded like Arthur.

I moved my head from side to side to locate the source, but I couldn't figure out where the voices were coming from. Were the debaters in the garden, or were their voices drifting from an open window?

"I won't need it for long," one of the men said, his words slurred, suggesting he was deep into his cups.

I missed the next sentence and hurried along the path to continue eavesdropping.

"How about half? You're good for it," the drunken man, who sounded a lot like Arthur, pleaded.

"I'll never see it again. Don't get into debt with me."

I stopped exploring the garden, no longer interested in the fresh air or my aching hip, and focused on the argument.

"Who's there?" a sharp female voice said from the shadows.

I jumped at the unexpected arrival. "Veronica Vale. Who's that?"

Emma Wainwright emerged from the gloom, her small dog on the ground. "I was walking Grace. I've had enough of all the noise in there. This was supposed to be a small, formal gathering, but suddenly, all and sundry turn up and cause chaos."

"I must apologise for intruding," I said.

"Not you. Although your pretty friend has the most grating laugh." Emma tutted as Benji trotted over. "I hope your dog behaves himself around Grace. She's sensitive, and doesn't like men."

"Benji's manners are impeccable." I watched Emma's dog as she sniffed noses with Benji. "You're not a fan of parties, I take it?"

"I don't mind a few friends, but it's out of control in there. Lady Sybil thinks she can recapture her lost youth by inviting Arthur's friends to these gatherings. Foolish woman. It's not respectable."

"It's good to surround yourself with bright young things now and again," I said.

Emma puffed out her disagreement. "You don't strike me as a bright young thing. And I can tell those shoes are hurting. You hobbled out here as if you were in your golden years. Although, I suppose neither of us is that far off being considered old maids."

"I have a few more good years in me." I lifted a foot and twisted my ankle around. "Borrowed heels. And I took a tumble today at a charity event for the dogs' home. I came away with a few bruises."

Emma sniffed. "How unfortunate. I admire your work with the dogs. It's a shame more people don't have time to give to them."

"If you have a few hours to spare, we're always looking for volunteers," I said.

She inclined her head, her gaze shifting to Grace. "I'll think about it."

We walked side by side, the dogs following us.

"I hope you don't mind me asking, but I recognised your name when Arthur introduced us. There's a reporter named Emma Wainwright. Would that be you?" I asked.

"Goodness! I'm astonished you've read anything I've written."

"I'm a journalist myself at the London Times. I like to keep a watch on other female journalists. There are so few of us, and we need to stick together."

"True enough, but our numbers are growing." The shrew-like expression on Emma's face softened. "I wrote a few pieces about women's rights back in nineteen fifteen, but I've had nothing published since April of the following year. Wainwright is my late husband's name."

"You stopped writing after he died?"

"No. When our parents died, I took a step back from my career to keep an eye on Arthur. As you may have noticed, he's not the brightest of chaps. And he has dreadful taste in women. I steer him when I can, but he mostly ignores my advice."

"That's decent of you." I did my best not to smile. Emma may not approve of Arthur's relationship with

Lady Sybil, but she was happy to stay in her beautiful home and drink her champagne.

"I had no other choice. Arthur lives in the moment. He cares little about how his actions will affect others. He accuses me of being stuffy, but one of us has to remain sensible."

"I suppose so. How long have Arthur and Lady Sybil been together?"

"Too long for my liking," Emma said. "Although I shouldn't complain. She is engaging company, and she invited several of us to stay the whole week. I'd never have been inside such an impressive home if it weren't for Arthur's connection to her."

"Providing they treat each other well and have the proper respect for each other, I see no problem with their relationship."

Emma stopped and glared at me. "If I wanted your opinion on my brother's inappropriate relationship, I would have asked. Good evening, Miss Vale." She scooped up Grace and marched away in her enviably flat black shoes.

I grimaced. I had a tendency to state my opinion even though it wasn't asked for, but Emma openly voiced her strong disapproval of Arthur being happy with Lady Sybil, so why shouldn't I offer a counter argument?

"Come along, Benji," I said. "Let's round this night off with a hot cup of tea and a snuggle in bed, shall we?"

His gentle bark suggested he considered that an excellent idea.

I kept the window down on the Ghost as I drove us back to London. I didn't want to risk falling asleep at the wheel, and the fresh air was bracing.

When I got home, I entered the house as quietly as I could. There was no sign of Matthew, but his bedroom door was closed, so he must have retired for the night. My mother was sound asleep, so I spent a few minutes tidying her room, removing the books from her bed, and placing a fresh glass of water on her bedside table. I smiled at the three cats snuggled in her blankets. Matthew had a fondness for cats and was always taking them in and nursing them back to health before finding them homes.

I pulled myself up the stairs, and as tempting as it was to drop onto the bed fully clothed and without washing the cosmetics off my face, I took a moment to remove my shoes, clothing, and makeup before flopping onto my soft pillows, rolling over in the covers, and falling asleep beside Benji.

My bedroom door hitting the wall jerked me out of a deep sleep, and I sat up, my eyes unfocused. Ruby landed on my bed. Her cheeks were tear-stained, and she grabbed my hand, squeezing it tightly enough to make me yelp. Todd's dog, Pippin, was with her, looking somewhat bemused.

"Whatever's the matter?" I asked. "Was it Peter? Did he behave inappropriately? Give me a minute to dress, and I'll pay him a visit with Benji. I'm sure Matthew will help, too. That rotter—"

"No! He was the perfect gentleman last night." Ruby's breath was ragged, and her pristine makeup was smeared around her eyes. It was most unusual. "Veronica, you have to help."

Benji whined and licked Ruby's free hand, before sniffing noses with Pippin.

"Of course. But you must tell me what's wrong." I failed to remove my hand from her bone-crushing grip, so I accepted the situation required such a firm squeeze.

"It's the worst news," Ruby said on a breathy sob. "Todd's been accused of murder."

Chapter 5

I stared at Ruby, and I kept staring until she pinched my arm, the pain bringing me to my senses.

"Did you hear me?" Ruby asked. "My brother stands accused of killing a man."

"Todd is no killer." I was still stunned and not yet fully awake to get my thoughts into order and say anything more detailed.

"That's what I've been telling the police ever since they informed me of this tragedy," Ruby said. "Your Inspector Templeton was kind enough to telephone me when he realised who he was dealing with."

I resisted the urge to tell her Inspector Jacob Templeton was very much not mine. It wasn't the appropriate time. "This makes no sense."

"Whatever's going on?" My mother appeared in the bedroom doorway, her dressing gown untied and her eyes bleary from sleep. "Oh! Ruby, was that you making all that racket?"

"I let myself in and knocked over the umbrella stand. I'm not thinking rationally. I'm so sorry to have awoken you."

"Hush your nonsense, child. You wouldn't come in here wailing and slamming things around if it wasn't serious." My mother moved with surprising speed, considering she was always trying to convince people she was a frail, bedbound old woman about to draw her last breath. She reached for Ruby and put an arm around her shoulder. "Tell me everything."

Ruby drew in a shaky breath, her tear-filled eyes fixing onto me. "It's my brother, Todd. The police have taken him because they think he murdered somebody last night."

"Murder!" Matthew appeared in the doorway in a set of striped pyjamas. He cuddled three kittens against his chest. "What's this all about?"

"If everybody would stop interrupting Ruby, we could find out exactly what is going on," I said. "Let's start with something simple. Why have you got Pippin with you?"

"Todd made me promise to look after her. Our parents are in Scotland, and he didn't trust any of his friends to care for her. Of course, I couldn't leave the poor little thing alone in his lodgings. Would you mind..." she held the lead out to me.

"Say no more. We'll take care of the dog," my mother said, "even though she'll plague my allergies and bring on another bout of pneumonia. What's going on with Todd?" She shuffled in beside Ruby and settled on the end of my bed, her arm still a protective shield around her. My mother's cuddles were always so reassuring.

"It's too dreadful to think of, but think of it, I must," Ruby said.

Matthew walked over and handed her a bundle of mewing fluff. "Kittens make the world feel like a better place. Take your time. There's no hurry."

"But there is! They arrested Todd an hour ago and took him in." Ruby kissed the kitten's head, a tear dropping onto its fur.

"Who do the police think he killed?" I asked.

"Arthur Buchanan!"

My eyebrows flashed up. "How? When? At Lady Sybil's party?"

"Who is Arthur?" my mother asked.

"An old school friend of Todd's," I said briskly. "He was involved with Lady Sybil."

"That's the wealthy widow you told me about?"

I nodded. "Ruby, we need the facts. How did Arthur die?"

"He was found in his bed," Ruby said. "And he didn't die at the party. He was discovered in a room at the Drunken Duck pub."

"Oh my! That's one of ours, isn't it? Or am I thinking of the Tipsy Toad?" My mother's gaze turned to me, since I managed the extensive list of pubs and inns my father had acquired over the years.

"Yes, it's in the village close to Lady Sybil's mansion," I said. "I'd planned to stop in before the party, but we ran out of time." The Drunken Duck pub had been a rundown building, empty for several years, but my father had renovated it into a thriving, popular village pub that drew visitors from the racecourse at Kempton Park. It had a thatched roof, low ceilings, and dark wood everywhere. It was a smashing little place and brought in excellent profits.

"Let's go back a few steps," I said. "Why wasn't Arthur staying at Lady Sybil's after the party ended?"

"I don't have all the information, but from what I understand from Inspector Templeton, Lady Sybil made Arthur leave the party. Apparently, he got drunk and embarrassed himself. Someone overheard her telling him to sleep it off and only return when he could behave respectably."

"He left the mansion and walked into the village," I surmised. "It's not too far. Although in the dead of night, it wouldn't have been pleasant. Why do the police think Todd is involved?"

"Inspector Templeton said someone overheard them fighting at the party. Todd threatened Arthur! Which is ridiculous. He'd never do such a thing."

"That doesn't sound like your brother," I said. "He's an easygoing chap."

"That's what I told Inspector Templeton! He said they were investigating the crime scene and would interview Todd shortly." Ruby's words wobbled out on another sob.

"Why is Inspector Templeton even involved in this case? Kempton Park is far from his usual patch," I said.

"Apparently, the chap who deals with murder in Kempton Park is sick, so Inspector Templeton was given the case. I'm so glad he was, or we'd be none the wiser until it was too late."

"I've met your brother, and he's a charming young fellow," my mother said. "The police must have the wrong man."

"I'll make tea, shall I?" Matthew had been standing awkwardly in the door with the other two kittens. He always wanted to help but was no good in a crisis, his ill health often flaring when he was under stress.

"Please. Make mine strong with plenty of sugar," Ruby said. "I'm in shock. I didn't know what to do when I received the telephone call."

Matthew hurried away to make himself useful.

"Where were you when you found out about Todd?" I asked.

"After you left, it wasn't so much fun. Peter was becoming pushy, and he wasn't as charming as I first thought, so I said goodbye to Lady Sybil around midnight, and she kindly arranged for me to be driven home." Ruby clasped my hand again. "Veronica, we must help Todd. He didn't do this."

"Of course we'll help him," I said. "We know Todd well enough to give him glowing character references. That'll stand him in good stead."

"What about the fight he had?" my mother asked. "Do you know what that was about?"

"Todd would never threaten anybody," Ruby said. "Whoever saw the disagreement must have mistakenly thought it was Todd. It must be someone else."

"We need more information." I slid out of bed and dressed hurriedly, making the best job of tidying my hair so I looked presentable before leaving the house. After a quick visit to the bathroom, I was ready.

"You can't go yet. You haven't had anything to eat," my mother said. "At least have a cup of tea or you'll faint on the street and be trampled."

I glanced at Ruby. She was pale and shaking. She wouldn't have even considered breakfast after receiving such shocking news. "A swift cup of sweet tea, but then we must be on our way. We'll go to the source of the information and discover what's going on. Then we can clear this matter up and get Todd free."

"Inspector Templeton will help," my mother said. "He's a kind man. And it's been an age since he dined with us. You must invite him over again."

"He was here barely a month ago. He had two servings of beef and ale pie," I said.

"I like a man with a hearty appetite. And with such a stressful job, he needs to find pleasure in the quiet moments."

Matthew came in with a tea tray laden with cups. We swiftly drank tea, and I fed Benji and Pippin, who, although seeming a trifle confused about her new surroundings, was getting on famously with Benji, and tucked into breakfast as soon as it was delivered.

"Mother, I'll leave Benji with you. He'll show Pippin the ropes and make sure she settles."

"Of course. I'll watch them both. Although my heart feels as if it's beating out of my chest with all these comings and goings. I need to go back to bed."

"I hope I haven't made you unwell," Ruby said. "I was so panicked when I got the news about Todd, and I knew Veronica would know what to do, so I came straight here."

"You're welcome anytime of the day and night." My mother rested a hand over her heart. "Just try not to bang the doors so loudly the next time a family member gets accused of murder."

"Let's hope there won't be a next time." I finished my tea. "Ready to go when you are."

Ruby set down her cup, handed the kitten to Matthew, and accepted a hug from my mother. After I'd told Benji he was a good boy and to look after Pippin, we were out the door.

It was a chilly Sunday morning, although there was a hint of sunshine, and it promised to be a pleasant day. The streets were deliciously quiet, most people still in bed, or preparing for church.

We hurried to Ruby's Ghost, which I'd carefully parked behind the house, and I climbed into the driver's side. Ruby must have still been in shock because she didn't pass comment that she wasn't behind the wheel. She loved to be in charge when it came to driving.

"I don't know what to make of this," she said after we'd driven the silent streets for a few moments. "Todd can be a blundering buffoon, but there's not a bad bone in his body. He always wants people to get along."

"This does seem remarkably out of character," I said. "Do you know if he had an issue with Arthur?"

"Todd doesn't have issues with anyone. He's everyone's friend. This must be a mistake. We'll speak to him and sort this matter out."

I swiftly navigated the streets, pleased there was barely any traffic, and we were soon parked outside the police station. We dashed inside to discover the place was empty, apart from a tired-looking policeman sitting behind the desk, and a man fast asleep on the cold concrete floor by the seats.

"We're here to see Inspector Jacob Templeton," I said.

The policeman barely had the decency to stifle a yawn behind his hand as he peered at us. "Who should I say it is? And what's the matter regarding?"

"Veronica Vale and Ruby Smythe. We're here about Arthur Buchanan's murder."

That prompted interest from the policeman, as murder usually does, and he telephoned through to Inspector Templeton. "He'll be out in a moment. Take a seat. Although watch out for Old Crankshaw. He passed out half an hour ago, and he's too heavy to move."

"Is he unwell?" Ruby peered at the snoring man.

"He'll feel like death warmed up given how much he had to drink last night." The policeman shook his head. "Stay out of his way, and he'll be no bother to you."

We waited five minutes before Inspector Templeton appeared. The tiredness beneath his eyes and his tousled dark hair suggested he'd had little sleep.

"I wondered when you'd make an appearance." He addressed me with that comment.

"I consider Todd a friend, so naturally, I want to ensure justice is done," I said. "You must know you have the wrong man."

Inspector Templeton let out a small sigh. "I am sorry about this, Ruby. I'm almost as surprised as you must be to find myself talking to your brother about such a serious matter. When I learned of the crime, I asked to be assigned to the case, so I could keep an eye on the situation. My superior had a few things to say about it, but I twisted his arm."

"Thank you, Inspector. What has Todd told you?" Ruby's voice had a small quiver to it.

"Very little. We've hit a roadblock," Inspector Templeton said. "Todd is refusing to talk until your family lawyer gets here."

"Which is perfectly acceptable," I said. "Todd is facing a murder charge."

"Yes, that's not the issue as such," Inspector Templeton said. "We contacted Basil Farnborough, but he declined the request to represent Todd."

"It can't be because he thinks he's guilty."

"Oh dear." Ruby's voice was unnaturally quiet. "I know what's going on."

"Then do tell, old girl," I said. "The sooner Mr Farnborough arrives, the sooner Todd will be free."

"Basil won't help because we have outstanding debts with his firm." Ruby's cheeks flushed. "I've been meaning to pay him, but there are always other expenses that come first."

"Don't worry yourself about that," I said. "I'll deal with the debt. Let's visit Todd."

Ruby looked like she was about to cry again, so I tucked her arm into my elbow and fixed Inspector Templeton with a stern look. "What are you waiting for? We have an innocent man to reassure."

He led us along a plain white corridor and opened the door to an interview room. We hurried in behind Inspector Templeton, to discover a bedraggled Todd slumped at the table, his head in his hands, and the scent of last night's alcohol lingering in the air.

"You have visitors," Inspector Templeton said. "Perhaps they'll encourage you to talk so we can untangle this situation."

Todd looked up, and his gaze brightened. He jumped from his seat and hugged Ruby first, then reached out an arm for me, too. As he embraced me, the scent of alcohol only intensified. How much had Todd had to drink last night?

"That's quite enough," Inspector Templeton said gruffly.

"I'll hug my brother for as long as I like." Ruby's words were muffled as her face pressed against Todd's shoulder.

"I'm doing fine, although it's chipper to see you both," Todd said. "I'm still getting over the shock of being dragged out of bed and told I killed someone, though. Can you believe it?"

"No! And you haven't killed anyone." Ruby stepped back from his embrace. Her eyes narrowed, and she thumped his arm. "Have you?"

Chapter 6

There were several minutes of debate between Ruby and Todd as they discussed whether to talk to the police. Todd repeatedly exclaimed his innocence, while Ruby told him to stop being a ninny and he had nothing to worry about.

I waited patiently beside Inspector Templeton, taking note of his tense expression. The look on his face gave me cause for concern. Perhaps he knew something Ruby didn't, some pertinent piece of evidence that implicated Todd in Arthur's murder.

Todd finally threw up his hands. "Very well! I'll talk if it will stop your nagging. I just didn't want to make a mess of things. I thought if I had Basil here, he'd get everything back to normal and make the police see sense without me putting my foot in it."

"Providing you say nothing foolish, you won't be arrested or charged with anything. Isn't that right, Inspector?" Ruby turned and looked at Inspector Templeton for confirmation.

"We are still in the beginning stages of this investigation. Given the evidence we've collected, we considered it prudent to bring Todd in at the earliest opportunity."

"I'll be interested to know what evidence you've collected," I said.

"So would I," Todd said.

"Let's take a seat and talk this through." Inspector Templeton gestured at the empty chairs.

Todd heaved out a sigh. "I will talk, but I'm confessing to nothing."

Inspector Templeton left the room for a moment and returned with another officer. He also brought in an extra chair so everyone could sit around the small table. Ruby sat next to Todd, holding his hand, while I sat on Todd's other side. Inspector Templeton and the other police officer faced us across the table.

Inspector Templeton checked his notepad, then focused on Todd. "Tell us more about the fight you had with Arthur on the night he was killed."

"There was no fight," Todd said, after a second of hesitation.

"Then explain the bruises and cuts on your hands and face."

Todd looked at his hands and grimaced. "I'll admit, they look bad, but I didn't get these injuries fighting with Arthur. Neither of us are fighting men. Well, was. Arthur wasn't violent. Neither am I."

"How did you get those cuts?" I asked. There were small gashes on several of Todd's fingers, and a torn nail on his right hand.

"From being, as my lovely sister often calls me, a ninny. I had too much to drink at the party. I went outside to clear my head, and I fell down some stone steps. I didn't see them since it was so dark. I thought I'd broken a bone, and lay there for a few minutes feeling sorry for myself. One of Lady Sybil's maids took pity on me and helped me up."

"Do you know the maid's name?" Inspector Templeton asked.

"Alice? Aggie? It began with an A. I'm not sure. Honestly, I was humiliated. The drink wasn't sitting right with me. My head ached, and I'd fallen over like an idiot. It was hardly an auspicious end to the evening."

"You need to get that information checked," I said to Inspector Templeton.

The officer sitting beside him made a startled noise and looked at his superior.

"Naturally, we will," Inspector Templeton said. "As I've mentioned, we are early in the investigation, but will cover all bases to ensure nothing is missed."

"It would be helpful if you told us what you already know," I said. "We may be able to eliminate Todd from your enquiries if the facts are laid out before us. Don't forget, Ruby and I attended this party, so we could fill in gaps in your knowledge."

Inspector Templeton flicked through his notepad several times while his colleague looked on in astonishment. "I suspect Ruby has already told you everything. I did request she be discreet, and I only contacted her as a courtesy because I recognised Todd's name when he was brought in."

"I have been discreet!" Ruby protested.

"I informed you what was going on, and at the earliest opportunity, you gossiped about it with your best friend," Inspector Templeton said.

"Veronica is the most discreet person I know," Ruby said. "She has to be in her line of work."

"You'll forgive me for saying that my experience suggests the opposite," Inspector Templeton said.

"Putting aside my indiscretions or otherwise," I refused to bristle at Inspector Templeton's impertinent words. "Perhaps you would be so kind as to let us know the facts you've gathered so far?"

Inspector Templeton mulled over the options before picking the right one. "Very well. We know Todd and Arthur attended the same party last night at Lady Sybil Montague's residence."

"And we were also there," Ruby said. "Todd provided us with an invitation."

"I know. We have a full guest list," Inspector Templeton said. "Lady Sybil has been very obliging."

"I left around ten fifteen that evening," I said. "And I saw no dispute between Todd and Arthur. Although..."

"There was something that concerned you?" Inspector Templeton asked.

"I overheard two men having a disagreement," I said. "It was just before I left. I didn't see them, but one of the voices sounded like Arthur. The conversation could have been about money."

"Who was the other man?" Inspector Templeton looked at Todd.

"I'm unsure. They were terribly drunk, so their words were unclear. It could have been anyone." I had wondered if the other man was Todd, but I'd been unable to see them, and refused to make things worse for Todd by suggesting he was involved in the disagreement.

"Was it you?" Inspector Templeton asked Todd.

"No! Our fight was about nothing."

"You admit you argued with Arthur at the party?" Inspector Templeton sat upright like a scent hound who'd caught a whiff of squirrel, his gaze alert. If he had a tail, he'd have pointed it behind him.

"I didn't say that! I... I had a lot to drink last night. My memory is hazy." Todd closed his eyes and massaged them with the tips of his fingers.

"I'd advise you to tell the truth," Inspector Templeton said. "We have spoken to other party guests, so the facts of the evening will reveal themselves, whether you want them to or not."

"Those facts will support my story," Todd said.

"Unfortunately, they're not."

Todd slumped in his seat. "Then whoever you're talking to is lying to you."

A tense silence filled the room, and unease settled in my stomach. Why was Todd being so prickly? Had something unpleasant occurred between him and Arthur? It was a challenge to keep an open mind when I knew the accused so well.

"I understand Arthur's body wasn't found at the party," I said to Inspector Templeton.

"It's the only reason I'm allowing you into this interview. Arthur's body was found in the Drunken Duck pub. An establishment I believe is owned by your family."

"It's a well-run pub with an excellent reputation. The landlady, Bridget O'Donnell, has been in the trade most of her life. She comes from a family of pub owners, and what she doesn't know about the business isn't worth knowing."

"We'll be speaking to the landlady in more detail shortly," Inspector Templeton said. "She found Arthur in his room less than two hours ago."

"Did Bridget tell you when Arthur arrived at the pub?" I asked.

"She knew exactly when he arrived. He thumped on the door until she came down and opened it. She wasn't best pleased to be woken at one thirty in the morning. It was only when Arthur paid her four times the nightly rate for the room that she let him in. It's a business practice I strongly discourage you from continuing."

"Daylight robbery," the attending policeman muttered.

"Providing they don't break the law, how my publicans run their establishments is their business," I said. "What time did Bridget find Arthur's body?"

"Seven o'clock. Apparently, Arthur asked for an early wake-up call. When he didn't respond, she went into his room and found him in the bed," Inspector Templeton said.

"Arthur died between approximately two and seven o'clock this morning," I surmised. "Did Bridget hear anyone else enter the pub between those hours?"

"She didn't hear a peep. Arthur was the only guest renting a room that night."

"Do you know what time he left Lady Sybil's party?" I asked.

Inspector Templeton's eyes narrowed a fraction, but he consulted his notepad. "He was seen stumbling away from the party just after midnight."

"Arthur was still there when I left, which wasn't long past midnight," Ruby said. "He seemed a little worse for wear, but by then, most people had had more than their fair share of Lady Sybil's fine champagne."

"Did you see Arthur arguing with anyone or unhappy?" I asked her.

"Veronica, if you please, this is my interview," Inspector Templeton said.

"I'm happy if Veronica asks questions," Todd said. "I want to figure this out as much as the rest of you. I know I didn't do this. Arthur was a friend, and I can't believe he's dead. We've known each other for years."

"Even so, this is a police investigation. Ruby is here because she is your family. Miss Vale is here because, once again, we discovered a body in one of her pubs," Inspector Templeton said.

"You make it sound as if bodies show up in my family's pubs all the time," I said.

He arched an eyebrow. "This isn't the first time an investigation has focused on one of your family's taverns."

I waved away his comment. "Let's focus on the case at hand. Arthur left Lady Sybil's party after midnight. The walk to the Drunken Duck would take maybe thirty minutes. Although if Arthur was excessively drunk, it could have taken him longer. Since he didn't arrive until gone one o'clock, we have to assume he got lost on the way."

"That tallies with what the landlady told us," Inspector Templeton said. "Arthur went to bed around one thirty."

I drew back my shoulders. "How was he killed?"

Inspector Templeton flipped his notepad closed. "Veronica! This is an active police investigation."

"Which you want to actively solve as soon as possible," I said. "And we want to clear Todd's name as quickly as possible, too. I won't publish the details you share, if that's your concern. But I insist on the facts so we can find the killer."

"That's our job, miss," the other police officer said.

"And you need our involvement because we are key witnesses," I replied. "Please. I'm not prodding because I want the thrill of the chase. Todd is innocent. And he's a friend. You'd do the same thing if the situations were reversed."

Inspector Templeton drew in a deep breath and let it out slowly, my plea for cooperation seeming to resonate with his conscience. "We've yet to determine the cause of death. As of yet, we can rule out knife wounds, guns, or any weapon that would cause obvious trauma to the body."

"Poison?" Ruby asked.

"That I can't tell you," Inspector Templeton said. "There were marks on Arthur's face and hands, very similar to those displayed by Todd."

"Arthur could have fallen, too," I said. "Country lanes are pitch black at night, and there are ditches on either side of the road. He could have slipped into one and injured himself."

"That's a possibility. It's also possible Arthur fought with someone just before he died and sustained the injuries that way."

"Not my brother," Ruby said.

"The witnesses we've spoken to revealed the fight between Todd and Arthur was explosive. Fists were used," Inspector Templeton said.

Ruby spun in her seat and glared at her brother. "Is this true?"

"I... I really couldn't tell you." Todd scrubbed the back of his neck with a hand. "I have a vague memory of arguing with someone. My head is so sore, though. I really shouldn't drink so much."

"Todd, I must ask this question. Did you kill Arthur in anger?" Inspector Templeton asked.

"No!" the three of us cried in unison.

"People must have seen Todd at the party after Arthur left," I said. "There's his alibi."

Todd shuffled in his seat and looked at his hands. "That's the tricky thing. The problem keeping me in this seat. I don't have an alibi."

"Why not?" I asked. "You didn't stay at the party?"

"I stayed for a short while, but I wasn't feeling good. You and Ruby had gone, Arthur had vanished, and I didn't know many other people. Then I had my fall and felt foolish, so I went for a walk. I just kept going. I found a park bench and slept on it for a while. I woke up a few hours later, cold and with an aching head. I got to a main road and found a taxi. It took me home, and that's when the police got me."

Ruby whacked him on the arm. "If our mother finds out about this, she'll be appalled. The shame will finish her. What if someone saw you and she discovers you were drunk and sleeping out in the open like you had no home to go to?"

"She won't die of shame if you don't tell her." Todd's expression grew anxious. "You're not going to, are you?"

"I should! She'd set you right."

"Please, don't bother her or Father. They're all the way up in Scotland, and you don't want them rushing back for no reason. By the time they return, this will be sorted."

"You can't keep a murder charge a secret for long." Inspector Templeton nodded at me. "The information will soon be made public in the newspapers."

"Not by me. And we can keep it secret because Todd is innocent," I said.

"I am!" Todd's bloodshot gaze darted around the room, desperation in his eyes. "I really didn't do it. Please, help me make this right."

Chapter 7

I'd telephoned Uncle Harry from the police station, given him a brief outline of the crisis, and informed him I'd be in late. He was understanding, but even so, I never liked to let him down. My job at the London Times was important to me, and I didn't want him to think I was taking advantage of the fact we were family.

After another hour with Ruby, I left her with Todd and caught a taxi to the newspaper office. I ignored Bob's snide comments about being late again and hurried into my uncle's office, closing the door behind me.

"I didn't expect to see you until this afternoon," Uncle Harry said, his tie slung over one shoulder and the top button of his shirt open. He looked very much like my father, and they had the same dark eyes.

"There's a mountain of obituaries to get through," I said. "And there was little I could do at the police station. Ruby is still with Todd, though. She refused to leave."

"It's a terrible business," Uncle Harry said. "I tapped into a few sources to see what I could find out, but it's all very fresh. Mainly rumours at the moment."

I nodded as I perched on the edge of the seat opposite my uncle. "Ruby's beside herself, and Todd's in shock.

I am, too! You never think a friend will be accused of something so ghastly."

"I've met Todd Smythe a few times at various functions. He never struck me as the type to snap. Many of the young men who've been to war come back different, though. They've seen dark things and faced terrible trauma. That changes a man."

"I don't disagree, but Todd never served. He has a heart condition, so he wasn't considered fit for duty."

"Well, that's good, in a way. It means his character won't be under too much scrutiny," Uncle Harry said. "It was a friend of his who died?"

"Arthur Buchanan. Todd is pleading innocence, but his case isn't helped by the amount of alcohol he had to drink. He has blanks in his memory."

Uncle Harry winced. "That's bad luck. My contact said there'd been a fight between Todd and Arthur."

I flashed up my eyebrows. "It seems you know almost as much as me."

Uncle Harry grinned and tapped the side of his nose. "I wouldn't be in this business if I didn't know how to cultivate contacts and gather information as quickly as possible. Today's news is tomorrow's fish and chip paper."

I sighed and massaged my forehead. "Todd admitted they had a disagreement, but he said it wasn't serious. He has worrying marks on his fists, though."

"You believe they came to blows?"

"Todd said he fell down some stone steps at Lady Sybil's home. I'll have to speak to the maid who helped him up, just to be sure."

Uncle Harry puffed out his cheeks. "Veronica, don't get too involved."

I stood, already feeling tired, and the day had only just begun. "Ruby's my best friend, and I consider Todd a friend, too. I'll stand by both of them. Now, I must get to work."

Uncle Harry shook his head. "On your own head, be it, my girl."

I settled at my desk, and I reached down to pat Benji. It always comforted me to feel his soft fur under my fingertips. Drat! Of course, I'd left him at home to watch Pippin and ensure she settled. I missed having Benji by my side. He was such a good boy and excellent company.

I looked through the dozen files of the recently deceased, ordered them in priority, then picked up the telephone. I wasn't placing a call to a family member to learn about their nearest and dearest, but instead, telephoned the Drunken Duck pub.

It was close to opening time, so Bridget would be busy setting up, but she was a reliable sort, so I hung on the telephone until it was answered.

"Kempton Park 3-5-7-9."

"Bridget, it's Veronica Vale."

"Hello, old duckie."

"I heard the bad news about one of our guests."

Bridget sighed heavily. "Bleedin' nuisance, if you'll pardon my French. Young man turns up his toes in my best room. I nearly had a heart attack when I discovered he was cold in the bed. Those sheets will need to be boil washed. Maybe I should just sling them."

"That must have been a shock," I said.

Bridget sniffed. "It's not the first dead body I've stumbled across. Hopefully, it'll be the last, though."

Bridget had a colourful past, and in her younger days, had worked as a lady of the night. My father had rescued her from an unpleasant encounter with a rough-handed sort and given her a job as a glass washer in the Drunken Duck. Her parents had run the place for years, but she'd fallen out of touch with them. My father reunited them, gave Bridget a job and a place to stay, and she learned everything she could about running a pub. When her parents passed, she took over the license and now ran a thriving establishment.

"The coppers are still here," Bridget whispered over the telephone. "I can't get rid of them. I had to call them when I found the body, but I hate them poking around and asking questions. Makes me feel guilty, and I've done nothin' wrong!"

"Cooperate as much as you can," I said. "I know you're not fond of the police, but they need to find out what happened to Arthur."

"I'll do my best, but I almost bit one of their heads off when he asked if I had anything to do with it. The cheek of the fella. Barely old enough to wear a uniform, and he's accusing a respectable lady of murder."

"I'm sure you set him right." I suppressed a smile. Bridget spoke her mind, no matter who she was talking to. It could be the Queen or a drifter, and she'd tell it like it was.

"I sent him away with a flea in his ear," Bridget said. "Some haughty inspector's been around asking questions, too. He spoke to me for half an hour. I kept telling him the same thing. After I let Arthur into the pub and took payment in full, I showed him to his room and left him to it. I'd been working all day, so I was exhausted. I went back to bed and fell straight to sleep."

"And you heard nothing?" I asked.

"As I kept telling the police, I saw Arthur to his room and was out like a light again five minutes later. I've always been a sound sleeper, although the brandy nightcap helped. I even used to sleep through the air raid sirens." Bridget made a loud noise like an old siren. "As you know, I'm always up early. I got up at six, made a cooked breakfast for me and Arthur, and took it up to him at seven as part of his wake-up call."

"Was his bedroom door unlocked?"

"Silly bugger hadn't locked it," Bridget said. "I knocked several times and told him his breakfast was ready, but he didn't reply. I checked the handle, and when it opened, I went in to give him a nudge. It was his job to lock himself in. I'm not to blame because he didn't listen to me."

"Of course, no one is blaming you," I said.

"I should think so, too. I had a bad feeling about him when he showed up so sloppy drunk, all sorry for himself. I should have turned him away, but it was late, and he seemed sad. He kept talking about a fight he'd had with his lady friend and how he embarrassed himself. I'm too soft-hearted. That's my trouble. And look where it's landed me. A body in my best bedroom, ruined sheets, and the coppers poking into my nooks and crannies."

"When you entered the bedroom, did you see anything unusual?"

"A dead body is unusual enough, isn't it?"

"I meant, did you see any signs of a fight? Had furniture been knocked over or damaged? And were there any signs of injury on Arthur's body?"

"You're a ghoulish sort, aren't you? I suppose you get used to the dead since you write about them all the time."

"The nature of my work does desensitise me somewhat," I said.

"Someone has to do it. And you write lovely obituaries. I read them out every day to my customers. You always make the dead sound interesting. Even the boring accountant you wrote about recently seemed like an interesting fella I wouldn't have minded stepping out with."

"I'm glad you like my work," I said. "Perhaps I'll write Arthur's obituary."

"Well, if you do, you'll do a grand job." Bridget was silent for a few seconds. "I saw nothing out of sorts in the room. All the furniture was untouched. I spoke to a copper—he was a chatty sort after I cooked him a sausage sandwich—and he mentioned suffocation could have done him in. Said since there was no blood on the body or on the bed sheets, it made sense the killer used a pillow to snuff Arthur out." She went quiet again. "And then there was the pillow itself. That's something strange, I suppose."

"What's that about the pillow?" I asked.

Someone tore one of my feather pillows. White feathers everywhere. Of course, it'll be muggin's here, clearing them up when the police finally leave. They're stamping them all over the place in their big boots."

"Maybe the killer tore the pillow to conceal evidence, or confuse the crime scene," I said, more to myself than Bridget.

"Reckon they might have. I saw a few marks on Arthur's hands, too. I didn't look for long, though, so I could have missed something. It gave me the creeps to see a body laid out all pale and unnatural like that."

"Arthur fought with someone last night," I said. "He could have gotten the marks during the brawl."

"That's important," Bridget said. "I've seen plenty of scuffles where they've both walked away, but one of the brawlers got a head injury. Finished him off later in his sleep."

"Goodness! I hadn't considered that. A head injury."

"It happens. I'm no expert, though. But I've seen plenty of fights and even been in a few, so I know to be careful if anyone's had a whack to the barnet and get a glazed look in their eyes. Never a good sign."

"Yes, that's something to consider." It was also something that had me worried. If Todd and Arthur had come to blows, maybe a fist went astray and Arthur received a damaging injury to his head.

"Anything else I can do you for? I've got the bottling up to finish."

"Are the police about ready to leave?" I asked.

"Not bleedin' likely. They look settled in for the day. They'll scare off my punters if they don't go soon."

"They're allowing you to open at lunchtime?"

"I will open at lunchtime. I don't care what anyone tells me."

"Try not to get yourself arrested, Bridget," I said.

She rasped out a dry laugh. "I'll do my best, duckie."

"I wanted to peek into the room, but I won't get an opportunity while the police are still there."

"Gawd! What do you want to do that for?"

"Well, it is my pub. And ... a suspect in the investigation is a friend."

"Blimey. Can't imagine you running around with criminals."

"I don't make a habit of it. It's Todd Smythe. Ruby's brother."

"I know the chap! Ruby, too, of course. What a surprise. He'd do nothing so evil." Bridget clucked out a few startled noises. "Still, you never really know a person. As for the room, the coppers won't let you look around, even if you put down ownership papers. They even discouraged me."

"I figured as much. But I need to get in there."

Bridget fell silent again, only her breathing informing me she was still on the line. "I hope you don't mind me saying this about your friend, but I get a lot of posh types in here. The racecourse has brought in a different crowd. I don't mind. They have plenty of money, but I've noticed a trend with some of them."

"What's that?" I asked.

"They can be deviant. Strange requests and interests. And some of them are downright rude. They get three strikes here, but if they don't watch their tongue, they're banned for life."

"I heartily approve of your management style," I said. "And although Todd and Ruby come from a wealthy background, I wouldn't class either of them as deviant. Although Ruby is horse obsessed. Would you consider that unusual?"

Bridget cackled a laugh. "I thought I'd put it out there. Get you thinking."

"Thoughts are appreciated at this stage," I said. "Please telephone me at the newspaper once the police have gone. I'd like to stop by as soon as possible."

"Will do, duckie."

We said our goodbyes, and I set the telephone back in its cradle.

"Not doing your job again, I see."

I'd been so engrossed in my conversation with Bridget that I hadn't heard Bob creeping up on me and snooping where he wasn't wanted. "I'm working very hard. Unlike some."

He lingered by my desk as I opened a file about a brick layer who'd been flattened in a most unsporting fashion. "A word of advice."

"I only take advice from those deemed worthy to give it."

Bob scowled at me, unsure if I'd just insulted him. "Don't chase this story because you think you can manipulate your connections. I cover murders in this newspaper."

"More like charity dog shows and garden parties."

"I wouldn't have been at that stupid dog show if your uncle hadn't twisted my arm," Bob said.

"At least you made sure to entertain yourself at my expense."

He chortled. "It was amusing to see you fall on your face and make an idiot of yourself."

"There's only one idiot here, and it most definitely is not me. Your irascible behaviour caused chaos."

"Someone needed to teach you a lesson," Bob said. "Stay out of this story. I'm doing the exclusive on this murder."

"I don't want to write about the murder," I said.

"Seems the opposite to me. You're poking around and asking questions you shouldn't be asking."

"And you're lurking around displaying a mind that functions at six guinea pig power." This wonderful insult had been reported in the newspapers after being delivered by Theodore Roosevelt to a slow-witted British ambassador. I adored it.

"That's enough, you two." Uncle Harry strode out of his office. "Everyone knows their roles in my newspaper. If Arthur's family asks, Veronica will write the obituary, so she'll need to gather useful information."

"And I'll write the story about how Arthur died," Bob said.

"Perhaps you will," Uncle Harry said. "But only if you give me five hundred words on the royal visit to Australia. And I'm still waiting for your write-up on the dog show. We need feel-good pieces in the newspaper."

"I'll be happy to provide a quote for the article," I said sweetly.

Bob grumbled to himself, stuffed his hands into his trouser pockets, and slumped off.

"Veronica." Uncle Harry drew out my name, his exasperation clear.

"Yes, Uncle Harry."

"Don't stir things."

"As if I would." I looked up at him and smiled. "You must come to dinner. Mother's been asking after you."

"Soon, soon. Too much work and never enough time." He leaned closer. "Do me a favour."

"Anything."

"Stop fighting with Bob. He can't match your intellect, and he gets angry when you make a fool of him."

"He picks fights with me! I must have recourse to retaliate."

Uncle Harry sighed. "Just do your job and stay out of trouble."

I stood and kissed him on the cheek. "When do I do anything else?"

Chapter 8

I worked through lunch, determined to catch up, and was getting to the bottom of my pile of files, when my desk telephone rang.

I picked it up, but before I'd drawn breath, the caller began talking.

"The very cheek of that man."

"Ruby! What's wrong?" I set down my pencil.

"Inspector Templeton evicted me from the police station," she said. "I'm having to use a public telephone box."

"Oh dear. What did you do?"

"Why do you assume it was me that was in the wrong?" Her tone was unnaturally shrill.

"Sorry, of course, you did nothing wrong. But why are you on the streets rather than inside the police station keeping an eye on Todd?"

"According to your Inspector Templeton, I was causing a scene."

"What exactly did that scene consist of?"

"I insisted on seeing Todd's cell and complained about the condition. There was paint peeling off the wall and a brown stain that I was certain wasn't your typical dirt.

I didn't approve of the lunch they brought him and offered to provide him with something edible. Then I mentioned the coffee was acidic and tasted burned. And then—"

"Ruby, it is a police station. You can't expect the accommodation to be luxurious."

"Todd is an innocent man, and they're treating him like he's guilty. His sandwich was stale! Stale! And the butter smelled iffy. They won't have stored it properly. He could get sick."

I held back a laugh. "I'll come and collect you. I don't suppose you've had anything to eat."

"I can't eat at a time like this! My foolish-headed brother is about to be charged with murder. Or die from eating a dubious sandwich. How can I trust the police to be competent when they can't even manage a decent cup of coffee or an edible sandwich?"

"Truly, those are dreadful crimes. I'm famished. I've not eaten all day."

"Golly! That's not like you."

"Exactly. These are stressful times. I need to make another telephone call and finish this obituary. I'll be with you in half an hour."

"I suppose I can find a bench and sit outside. At least the sun is out. Poor Todd, he may never see the sun again if we don't fix things."

"Even if the worst happens, prisoners get regular outdoor exercise. He'll have a lovely concrete yard to trudge around."

"Veronica! Don't say such dreadful things. And hurry. Your talk of food has made my stomach growl, and its most embarrassing. There's a gentleman waiting to use the telephone who is looking at me strangely. He must think I have a creature hidden under my coat. Oh! There it goes again. Mortifying."

"I'll be as quick as I can." I ended the call, then contacted the operator and took down the telephone number for Basil Farnborough.

"Mr Farnborough, this is Veronica Vale. You don't know me, but I'm a friend of one of your clients. This is regarding the Smythe family."

"Miss Vale. How may I assist you?" Basil had a nasally voice and an air of disinterest in his tone.

"You're aware of the unfortunate situation Todd Smythe has found himself in?" I asked.

"Mr Smythe has contacted me. I am unable to take his case."

"Because of an unpaid debt," I said. "Allow me to pay it. I can stop by your office with the money."

There was a pause. "If the debt is cleared, I'm happy to take on the case. It is a significant sum, though."

"It's no matter. Give me the details, please." I jotted down the amount, my eyebrows flashing up at the number he gave me. "I shall withdraw the funds and be with you presently."

"I look forward to meeting you."

I set down the telephone and hastened through my work. Once I was satisfied the dead had been appropriately attended to, I collected my things, said a quick goodbye to Uncle Harry, then dashed out of the office. I hailed a taxi which took me first to my house so I could pick up Benji, as I was missing him dreadfully. A quick check on Pippin showed she was sound asleep and comfortable, so I was confident about leaving her at the house. Then I went to my bank, withdrew the funds required to pay the debt, and deposited the money in the hands of a surprised-looking Basil Farnborough, who reminded me of a disgruntled toad caught in a bright light.

After that, it was a whirlwind dash to the police station to discover Ruby sitting on a bench, looking most aggrieved. I paid the cabbie and asked him to wait, then climbed out of the taxi, beckoning her over.

"I was beginning to think you'd forgotten me," Ruby exclaimed. "You said half an hour."

"I could never forget you," I said. "Look lively, the taxi's waiting. And I know just the thing to lift our spirits."

"You've found Arthur's killer?" Ruby dashed over, and we settled into the taxi. "That's the only thing that will cheer me up."

"Not yet. But there's a marvellous tearoom opposite the Drunken Duck."

Ruby's eyes widened. "Oh! I would die for a cream tea."

"Then that's what we shall have." I gave directions to the driver, and he soon left the busy streets of London, heading through leafy suburbs, before cruising into the attractive village of Much Mallow and pulling up outside Mrs Patterson's Tearoom. It was a pretty white building with bunting in the window and yellow flowered curtains.

Ruby's gaze went across the street to the Drunken Duck pub, and she frowned. "This is where all of Todd's troubles began."

"And where Arthur's ended," I said. "Before we talk over the suspects, we need fuel."

Ruby made no protest as I escorted her into the tearoom. I'd been here many times when visiting the pub, and Mrs Patterson was dog-friendly, so Benji came in too. I ordered two deluxe cream teas, and we settled at a table by the window, not close to other customers so our conversation wouldn't be overheard. The spot also gave us an excellent view of the pub, and it was plain to see the police were still in residence.

"How is Todd faring?" I asked Ruby.

"He has a stiff upper lip, but I can tell he's terrified. The poor lamb. I'm trying to reassure him, but his head is in a muddle."

"Everyone had rather too much to drink at that party," I said.

"Well, the champagne was excellent. I must admit, I'm not feeling my best."

Mrs Patterson bustled over with a large pot of tea and two china teacups with saucers that had matching flower patterns around the edge. "I suppose you ladies heard about the goings-on over the road."

"Naturally, since it's one of my concerns," I said.

"You must know the latest, then." Mrs Patterson crossed her arms under her ample bosom and waited for me to share the gossip.

"I'm very much in the dark about current events," I said. "I was hoping to get access to the pub, but the police are still there."

"They don't seem keen on leaving," she said. "I had a couple in here for lunch. All they said was there's been an incident and a young fella lost his life."

I nodded. "It's a tragedy."

Mrs Patterson waited for me to continue, then frowned when I remained silent. "You don't know anything else?"

"We're leaving it in the police's capable hands." Ruby's voice didn't betray an ounce of cynicism.

"Locals should be kept informed," Mrs Patterson said. "I won't be able to sleep soundly knowing there's a killer skulking around out there. Although one of the policemen mentioned they'd already caught the chap who did it."

"They absolutely have not!" Ruby said. "That's stuff and nonsense."

I kicked her under the table. "I'm sure the police know what they're doing."

Mrs Patterson glanced from Ruby to me, sensing we were concealing information. "Maybe they do. They brought the body out not so long ago. I couldn't see who it was since he was covered."

That was handy news. The body had gone, so the police would soon follow. "You have nothing to worry about. It's most unlikely the killer would remain in the village for fear of being caught."

"You can never be too careful. I'll be double-checking my doors and windows tonight." Mrs Patterson bustled off and came back a moment later with a tower of treats on a beautiful cake stand. There were freshly made scones nestled beside a pot of strawberry jam, and a large dish of rich clotted cream. On the second tower were a dainty selection of delicious-looking cakes, and on the bottom layer, finger sandwiches containing smoked salmon and cream cheese, prawn mayonnaise, beef and mustard, and cheese and tomato.

Ruby's face brightened at the feast, and after thanking Mrs Patterson, we tucked in.

Neither of us spoke for several minutes as we enjoyed the food. Ruby went for a scone, smothering it in cream and jam and taking an enormous bite. I made up a small plate of food suitable for Benji, and set it down for him, before taking my own scone. After all, they looked delicious. Dessert was often the best part of any meal.

Once we'd filled our stomachs, I pulled out my notepad and flipped it open. "I've been thinking about suspects."

"So have I. I tried to talk to Todd about who killed Arthur, but he kept getting distressed and saying it wasn't him." Ruby kept her voice low to avoid being overheard by Mrs Patterson. "I had to flick his ear several times to get his attention."

"I know you'll hate his name being on the list, but we must look at this as if we were the police. For now, Todd must remain a suspect."

Ruby's brow furrowed as she stuffed the last piece of scone into her mouth and chewed furiously. "I don't like it. He's innocent."

"I agree, but the police think otherwise. They're looking for evidence to implicate him."

"Which means we must look for evidence to prove the opposite."

"We will. So, other suspects. How about Lady Sybil?"

Ruby dabbed at her mouth with a napkin and selected a prawn mayonnaise sandwich. "I don't know her character well. She moves in exclusive circles that are sadly beyond me."

"Same here," I said. "But she seemed a respectable sort, although not overly friendly when we arrived at her party. Someone who enjoys fun within the boundaries of social mores."

"A murder would smash through those boundaries."

"She did argue with Arthur," I said. "She made him leave the party. That must have been a humiliation. Lady Sybil may be genteel, but if she's one to hold a grudge, she may have decided to go after Arthur to sort things out."

"If she found him at the pub, he would have had no objections about letting her into his bedroom," Ruby said. "He probably hoped for some naughty fun!"

"I found out something useful from Bridget when I telephoned the pub," I said. "Arthur didn't lock his bedroom door. Anyone could have gotten in and attacked him."

"That's unlucky," Ruby said. "If he'd locked himself in, he'd still be alive."

"Most likely." I chose a cheese and tomato sandwich and set it on my plate. "We need to find out what Lady Sybil and Arthur argued about. Perhaps Arthur tried to break things off, or Lady Sybil caught him having a dalliance with another woman and didn't like it."

"Yes, she's definitely a top suspect," Ruby said. "Who else?"

"Arthur's older sister was at the party," I said. "Emma Wainwright."

"I barely saw her," Ruby said. "Apart from when we were introduced. She didn't strike me as friendly."

"I met her in the garden before I left," I said. "She's a no-nonsense woman. Perhaps Arthur's tomfoolery got too much for her."

"She seems too prim to be a murderess," Ruby said. "But we should check her alibi."

"What about your new friend Peter Appleby?" I asked. "You know his character better than me."

Ruby's nose wrinkled. "I'm not sure I do know his true character. When I was getting to know him, he was charming, attentive, and an excellent dancer. But as the night wore on, his mood changed. It could have been the drink that made him uncouth, but I didn't like what I was seeing. It was why I left."

"He was good friends with Arthur," I said. "But perhaps they had a falling out. He could have been the man I heard Arthur arguing with when I was in the garden."

"Peter must be on the suspect list, too," Ruby said. "Perhaps Arthur confided in him as to where he was going after Lady Sybil threw him out. If they'd argued earlier in the evening, Peter could have still been angry and pursued him."

I wrote Peter's name then set down my pencil. "Ruby, there's no easy way to say this, and you know I adore Todd, but he has an impulsive nature."

"I know that! I grew up with the ninny. But being impulsive doesn't make him a killer."

"No, but it makes him act irrationally," I said. "When I spoke to Bridget, she wondered if a punch had gone astray and done damage to Arthur. Maybe he sustained an injury which was fatal but didn't kill him until later that night."

Ruby dropped her half-eaten sandwich onto her plate, and tears filled her eyes. "No! I can't believe it. Todd's not a fighter. He gets out of breath when I make him walk fast. He has no stamina."

"I'm not saying he's guilty, but we must consider all the possibilities. The police will look at that angle too when they conduct the autopsy."

"What do we do? What if it was a stray punch? What a terrible prospect."

I reached over and squeezed her hand. "We find Todd a solid alibi to prove his innocence. If there was no way he could have been at the Drunken Duck when Arthur was murdered, he'll be in the clear."

Ruby sighed. "If only park benches could talk."

"Maybe the bench Todd slept on can't talk, but someone must have seen him that night." I looked at the pub. "Since the police don't seem eager to leave, we'll finish our cream tea and take a walk. The village park isn't far from here. And you never know. We may find the perfect bench to sit on and the perfect person to talk to."

Chapter 9

A brisk walk was just what we needed after consuming the deluxe cream tea. I strode along, admiring the pretty thatched cottages and quaint small-windowed houses in Much Mallow. Ruby was speeding along beside me, her heels tapping on the pavement.

"Steady on, or I'll get a stitch if we keep up this pace."

"The exercise will do you good," I said.

"It won't in these shoes."

"Don't you want to hurry and clear your brother's name?"

Ruby poked me in the arm with a sharp elbow. "Don't use my brother's foolishness to force me to exercise. I get quite enough physical exertion riding Lady M's horses."

"Have you told her the news about Todd?" I slowed slightly since Ruby had begun to wheeze.

"I telephoned her when I knew she'd be awake. She's not the earliest of risers. I didn't give her all the details, but I said there was a family emergency and I wouldn't be in work for several days."

"And she was happy?"

"Not particularly. But for all her abruptness, she's a decent sort. She told me to look after myself and she'd hire a retired jockey friend to ride the horses until I return. It's not necessary, since there's a regular stable hand who's very capable. Lady M does have a thing for short men in tight clothing, though, so perhaps she wanted a stimulating view."

"We all have a particular type." I pointed ahead of us. "There's the park."

"Jolly good. All we need to do now is find the right bench and hope it reveals its secrets."

The village park was pleasant, not large, but well maintained, with neat flower beds and tidy grass. A circular path weaved around the edge, and we chose that route, which gave us a full view of the park's facilities.

There were six benches, and we examined them all, but there was no evidence Todd had fallen asleep on any of them.

A small group of men sat on the grass as if engaged in a late afternoon picnic. Although their grubby overcoats and scruffy beards suggested they may not have homes in the village. Or homes at all.

"Perhaps the local residents will be able to help," I said.

"Be careful," Ruby said. "They don't look friendly."

"One of them has a dog. Any man who spends time with a dog has to have a good character. Follow me. If we get into trouble, Benji will protect us."

Benji wagged his tail, but behind his affable cuteness, rested a heart full of courage and loyalty.

We strode to the four men, who looked up as we approached. As I suspected they would, they had bleary eyes, and several clutched bottles of alcohol. I greeted the men and introduced ourselves while Benji headed to the dog, and they engaged in a typical dog greeting.

"We are in need of help," I said.

"I doubt there's anything we've got that will help you, missus," one of the men said. "Unless you're looking for a slug of cheap gin."

The others chuckled.

"It's a little early for me," I said.

"Not me," Ruby said, "although I shouldn't. I need to keep a clear head."

"You don't want to drink any of this," a grey-bearded man said. "You'll go blind. We brew it ourselves."

"How ingenious," I said. "Do you regularly visit this park?"

"Most days, when the weather is nice. Even when it isn't so nice, when the shelter's full."

"Then you're who we need to speak to. Did any of you see a young man asleep on a park bench two nights ago? He has dark hair longer than the current fashion, and he was wearing a smart suit."

"We know nothing about that."

The men turned away and hunched over.

"It would help us so much if you saw him," Ruby said. "He's my brother, and he's gotten himself in trouble."

"He must have been in trouble if he slept in our park." The grey-bearded man appeared to be the group's spokesperson.

"Please! We need your help," Ruby said.

The men remained gruffly silent, although a couple of them slid Ruby an apologetic look.

I crouched close to the dog in their company. He had an injured paw and was holding it off the ground. "Is your dog friendly? It looks like he could do with some assistance."

"He's friendly enough if you're friendly to him." The man with the grey beard glanced at me. "I'm worried about that paw. It's been troubling him for days."

"I can help. I've had dog companions most of my life. They're always getting themselves into scrapes and needing a little extra care."

The man swivelled around and fully faced me. "I always make sure he's fed, but he likes to roam. And people are messy. They leave old tins and broken glass around."

"Do you think he stepped on something?" I gently examined the dog's paw. He whimpered but remained placid. He was a handsome chap, with short tan fur and pointy ears.

"There's a cut on one paw. I wash it every day, and I tried to get a bandage on it, but he tugged it off with his teeth. Daft beggar."

"Have you taken him to see a vet?" There was a deep cut on the paw, but no signs of infection.

"Where can I get the money for that? I can barely feed the two of us and have enough for a bed at the shelter. Not that the place is much warmer than being out here when the weather is good."

"Do you know about the dog's home in Battersea?" I asked.

He twisted a strand of his coarse beard. "It's a way from here."

"It is. I volunteer there, and once a week, we have a free treatment day for people who struggle with their finances."

"I don't take charity."

"But you want a dog who is healthy and happy, don't you?" I asked. "I could arrange for you to visit. It would be in the best interests of this lovely boy."

The grey-bearded man grunted and gently patted the dog. "I could make an exception for him. Free, you say?"

"Once a week, every Thursday. Local vets volunteer their time at the dogs' home. You should visit. Neither of us wants to see your dog miserable."

The man took a drink from the bottle he held and grimaced. "We'll be there."

"Excellent. Let me jot down a few details so they know who to expect." I pulled out my notepad and pencil. "You've done a marvellous job of keeping the paw clean. Thanks to you, there is no infection, so he'll heal nicely."

"I'd do anything for him. He looks out for me, so I look out for him." The man's tired eyes glittered with unspoken affection.

I took down the details of the dog, but could only get the name Thomas from the homeless man. I tucked away the information and assured him I'd be happy to see them this Thursday, and gave him enough coin to travel on the bus.

"I suppose this means I owe you a favour," Thomas said.

"If your memory has been jogged regarding the young man we were asking about, I'd consider the favour instantly repaid."

His friends grumbled out words of caution, but one of them nodded at him.

"We saw the man you were asking about. A posh type splayed out on the bench over there." He pointed to the opposite side of the park.

"You really saw him!" Ruby clasped her hands together. "Todd was here?"

"I didn't ask him his name, since he was in no fit state to talk," Thomas said. "He stumbled into the park talking to himself, then sang to a bush, got to the bench, and collapsed. He had on a smart suit like you said, and shiny shoes. Had that messy hair, too."

"Do you remember what time he arrived?" I asked.

The group consulted among themselves.

"Hard to say for sure," Thomas said. "It was late. We'd been asleep for a while, when he disturbed us. I'd say one o'clock."

"Did you see Todd leave?" Ruby asked.

"It was impossible to avoid! He was moaning and groaning when he got off that bench. No surprise, they're not comfortable to sleep on. That was around four-thirty. He headed towards the main road. He wasn't singing anymore, though." Thomas chuckled to himself.

"He didn't go towards the pub?" I asked.

"No, the opposite way. I imagine he had a sore head and wanted his bed."

Ruby grinned. "This is perfect. This information means Todd is in the clear."

After our delicious afternoon tea and conversation with Thomas and his friends in the park, I'd returned to work for a few hours. I'd wanted to continue the investigation, but my uncle's patience would only stretch so far if I kept taking extended time away from my desk.

Ruby had decided some late afternoon shopping was in order to boost her spirits, and we'd agreed to meet back at the police station at six that evening with the news for Inspector Templeton about Todd's innocence.

"What's keeping him so long?" Ruby tapped her fingers against her knee. We were in the waiting room of the police station and had been there for ten minutes after requesting to see Inspector Templeton.

"Remember to be on your best behaviour," I murmured. "You don't want to be thrown out on the street again, do you?"

"I was making a stand for the wrongly accused," Ruby said. "You always do that, and you never get treated the way I did. And we know the reason why."

"Do we now?"

Ruby arched a well-groomed eyebrow. "Your Inspector Templeton allows you to take liberties."

"If you keep calling him my Inspector Templeton, you'll start untrue rumours. We know what the man thinks of me."

A smile tracked across Ruby's face. "Refresh my memory. Despite his surly manner, he can be pleasant company, and he is extremely attractive, even when scowling."

"Then, my dearest Ruby, you date the man."

She waved away my comment. "He's not the chap for me."

"Too reliable? Has a good job? Doesn't break the law?"

"Behave yourself! I consider Inspector Templeton like a brother. An annoying one, but I have not a single romantic inclination towards him."

I wrinkled my nose at that description of the inspector. "He allows me to linger around cases because I'm useful. So are you when focused. He won't admit it, but we've been enormously helpful to him in the past."

Ruby crossed her arms over her chest. "And do we get any credit?"

"The reward money for solving Florence Sterling's murder was appreciated," I said. "The dogs had a marvellous time with their new toys, and we won't have to worry about the funds to buy their food for months."

"That's a comfort of sorts," Ruby said.

The door opened, and Inspector Templeton appeared. His eyes narrowed when he saw Ruby. "I trust we won't have any more problems, Miss Smythe?"

"I won't make a peep," she said. "Veronica has told me to behave, so behave I shall."

"Ruby is almost as well trained as Benji." I got a jab in the ribs for that comment.

"We don't need added complications. We're all busy and doing our best," Inspector Templeton said.

"Tell that to the person who makes the sandwiches," Ruby muttered to me under her breath.

"You have information pertinent to your brother's case?" Inspector Templeton asked her.

"Perhaps we could see Todd and give you the information at the same time?" I stood from the hard chair.

"Here will do. As I've already said, we're extremely busy."

Oh dear. We had the grumpy version of Inspector Templeton this evening. "Very well. We found witnesses who saw Todd in Much Mallow Park. He couldn't have murdered Arthur at the pub."

Surprise flashed across Inspector Templeton's face. "Who are these witnesses?"

"Local villagers," I said. "They enjoy being outdoors at all hours."

"You mean, the beggars who spend their time drinking homemade spirits and making a nuisance of themselves?"

"How do you know about them?"

"Because I'm excellent at my job. And when I interviewed them no less than an hour ago, they were full of news about two posh ladies with a dog. One of them said you gave him money."

Blast! Our snooping had been uncovered. "For the bus fare, so he could take his own dog to the vet. I'm glad you're being so thorough in your investigation. I trust they informed you Todd was in the park that night. He slept on the bench until four-thirty and then went in the opposite direction to the pub when he left."

Inspector Templeton sighed and shook his head. "Drunk, homeless men are unreliable witnesses. Any statements we collect won't stand up in a court of law."

"They seemed barely drunk to me," Ruby said. "Merely a touch merry. Most of them were gruffly friendly."

"Then you weren't being observant," Inspector Templeton said. "How do I know, since you got to them first, that you didn't offer them those coins to say they saw Todd in the park?"

"How very dare you," I said. "As if we'd do such a despicable thing."

"You'd do it to save Todd," Inspector Templeton said.

I scowled at him. "We know how the law works. We wouldn't break it to get a false statement. That would only make things look worse for Todd."

Inspector Templeton pinched the bridge of his nose and closed his eyes for a second. "I suspect you're telling the truth, but my statement stands. Those men are unreliable witnesses. When this case goes to court—"

"When it goes to court," Ruby said, "Todd will not be there accused of murder."

"I hope that's the truth," Inspector Templeton said. "I'm really sorry, but as things stand, all evidence we've collected makes it seem likely Todd killed Arthur."

A sob escaped Ruby's lips, and she pressed a fist against her mouth.

I placed a comforting hand on her shoulder. "What about the other suspects? Lady Sybil? Emma Wainwright? Peter Appleby? There were other people at the party who had a grudge against Arthur."

"You want to pin this murder on Lady Sybil?" Inspector Templeton shook his head. "You're stretching because you're desperate."

"I'm offering you options! You need to get off the one-track thought that Todd Smythe is a killer."

"Let me offer you something else." Inspector Templeton strode to the door and opened it. "It's time for you ladies to go home."

I stared at him in disbelief. "You can't make us leave."

"I'd like to see Todd," Ruby said. "I know my rights."

"Clearly not. No visitors at this time. Come back tomorrow." Inspector Templeton opened the door wider.

After a brief staring competition, I admitted defeat. He wasn't budging, and as reluctant as I was to back down, I knew when to pick my battles. A tired, belligerent man who needed sleep wasn't worth troubling.

I headed outside with Ruby, and we stood for a few moments on the busy pavement, watching the cars and open-top buses idle past in the traffic.

"What do we do now?" Ruby asked. "We presented the evidence, and Inspector Templeton dismissed us. It makes me think he wants to find Todd guilty."

"I know what we'll do." I caught hold of Ruby's elbow and steered her towards her car. "We go back to the Drunken Duck, and find the clues the police missed."

Chapter 10

An hour later, we were settled at a small round wooden table near the open fireplace in the Drunken Duck. The pub was busy, and Bridget was dashing around behind the bar, serving her regulars. We already had refreshments. Ruby was sipping on a dry martini, while I had a small gin and bitters.

"Sorry to keep you, ladies." Bridget hurried over. "The locals want to gossip about what happened upstairs. Gruesome bunch."

"It's only natural," I said. "In fact, that's why we're here."

"Of course." Bridget leaned down and hugged Ruby. "I'm sorry to hear your brother's involved in this muddle."

"Thank you." Ruby looked teary-eyed as Bridget released her from the hug. "We're determined to clear his name."

"Good for you." Bridget slapped a hand on the table. "Now, I can't have you ladies drinking on an empty stomach. I've got my pie and mash special tonight. It's always popular."

I shouldn't have been hungry after eating the enormous cream tea, but I'd eaten Bridget's pies before and they were always scrumptious. I looked at Ruby and raised my eyebrows.

"I could eat," she said.

"I'll get your food ready, and while you wait, you can nip upstairs. See the scene for yourself," Bridget said. "The police said I wasn't to let anyone up there, but this is my pub, so I'll do as I please. And if they question me about it, I'll say my terrifying boss insisted on having a look."

I smiled warmly at Bridget. "Feel free to misuse my name to avoid trouble."

"The food won't be long. I'll give you the key to the room. But keep it discreet. You don't want anyone sneaking up behind you to take a look." Bridget grabbed the key from behind the bar and handed it to me with a wink.

I knew the way through the pub, and we ascended the stairs. It was a small building, and there were only four guest rooms on the upper level, with two doors on either side of the corridor. I slotted the key into the first guest room and unlocked it.

We stepped into a quiet, tidy space. The bed had been stripped. The curtains had yet to be drawn over the window, and there was a small dressing table and wardrobe.

"It's hard to imagine Arthur died in here," Ruby said softly. "The room seems so normal."

"It does. Although it now makes sense that Bridget heard nothing unusual. Her room is at the far end of the corridor."

Benji trotted around the room, sniffing. He seemed relaxed and content, so I let him explore while we walked a circuit. There was nothing out of the ordinary on display. The dressing table drawers were empty, and so was the wardrobe.

Benji wriggled under the bed, and after a moment, he came out. He had several feathers attached to his fur.

"These must have come from the torn pillow." I plucked the feathers off Benji and patted him.

Ruby peered under the bed. "There's nothing under there apart from a few more feathers."

"It would have been most handy if the killer had left a signed confession to find," I said. "There's nothing of use in here."

We walked around the room one more time, just to be certain.

"Whoever did this could have broken into the pub," I said. "There should be evidence of how they gained entry."

"Unless Bridget left a main door unlocked," Ruby said. "If that happened, there'd be no obstacles to the killer getting to Arthur."

I looked out of the window. "It would have been hard to scale up from down there, so they must have come through a downstairs door. We'll inspect all the windows, though, in case anyone used a ladder."

Ten minutes later, and we discovered no broken or damaged windows on either floor. There was only one option left.

We returned to the pub, and our timing was perfect because Bridget was bringing out two huge plates of steaming pie and mash, which she proudly set down in front of us along with our cutlery. "That'll put hairs on your chest."

"This looks incredible," I said. "If I eat all of it, I won't need to worry about dinner for a week."

Bridget chuckled as she set a bowl of beef chunks down for Benji. "I like to make sure my customers are well fed and happy."

"Have you got a minute to join us?" I asked. "We've got a few questions about ... you know what."

Bridget glanced at the bar and nodded. She grabbed a chair and settled in.

"Could you talk us through what happened when Arthur arrived?" I asked.

"I've already told you everything. He was hollering and banging on the door like a man possessed. I took pity on him and let him in. And I'll confess, I charged an excess for the room. It's all done proper, though, and will go through the books."

"I don't doubt your honesty for a second," I said. "Walk us through your exact steps. You heard Arthur and came down here. Then what did you do?"

"I unlocked the door. I had to grab him to stop him from falling on his face, foolish man."

"And then what?" I scooped up gravy-covered mash, blew on it, and took a bite. It was wonderful.

"I made sure he was steady on his feet and then closed the door. We negotiated for a minute and agreed on the rate. Then I got him his key and showed him to his room. That was it."

"Did you lock the main pub door?" I asked.

Bridget's cheeks flushed. "I can't say for certain. It was late, I was tired, and I wasn't happy about being disturbed. I just wanted to get back to my bed."

"We're figuring out how Arthur's killer got into the pub," I said. "If you left the main door unlocked, they could have snuck in."

Bridget heaved out a sigh and picked at a nail. "Maybe I left it unlocked. But it's not my fault Arthur got killed."

"Of course. I'm not looking to blame you," I said.

"Absolutely not," Ruby said. "But we need the facts. By the way, this pie is delicious."

"Thank you. I do feel a touch of guilt. If I'd pushed the bolt for certain, the killer wouldn't have gotten in. I told the police everything, though. They know I may have left the door open."

"Once again, you aren't to blame," I said. "Arthur also left his bedroom door unlocked."

"Bad luck all round," Ruby said.

"I'm dying of thirst over here, Bridget," a man yelled from the bar, holding up his empty pint glass.

"Keep your hair on. I'll be with you in a minute. I hope that was useful. And I hope you get things sorted for your brother," Bridget said to Ruby, before rising from her seat and dashing to the bar.

Ruby set her fork down, having made a hearty dent in the pie. "Although the visit to the bedroom wasn't useful, we now know how the killer got to Arthur."

I nodded as I finished my mouthful of mash. "It's progress, but we must move quickly and get to the other suspects fast before Inspector Templeton charges Todd with Arthur's murder."

Yesterday had been eventful and busy, so I was glad to have a relaxed breakfast with my mother and Matthew. Mother was in bed as usual, and I reclined on the end with Matthew on the other side while we enjoyed hearty bowls of porridge. I'd been updating them as to Todd and Arthur's situation.

My mother's hand fluttered against her chest. "It makes my heart pound with worry, thinking if a nice young man like Todd Smythe could become a killer, we're all done for."

"Todd isn't a killer." I reached down and patted Benji and Pippin, who sat obediently by the side of the bed, waiting for treats.

Matthew shook his head, his hair its usual tousled mess and his pyjamas misbuttoned. "I can't believe Todd did it. He comes from a good family."

"A poor family, though," my mother said. "I heard Mrs Smythe recently had to sell her wedding ring."

"Where did you hear such nonsense?" I asked.

My mother shuffled under her blankets, looking vaguely contrite. "Sally overheard someone talking in the launderette about the Smythe family being down on their luck. Although, she also said they can afford to go on holiday to Scotland, so they can't be that poor. I suppose some people have different priorities when it comes to money."

"Mother! Don't let Ruby hear you talk like that. Maybe they are having a few financial difficulties, but they'll make things right. Ruby and Todd's parents have gone to Scotland because of a work opportunity they couldn't afford to turn down."

Mother didn't look convinced. "If you say so."

"I do. I also say it's time for me to leave. I've got my first appointment with a suspect soon."

"Suspect! Don't visit any killers." Mother's face paled. "What if they attack you?"

"Lady Sybil is one of the most refined murder suspects I've ever happened across." I passed my empty porridge bowl to Matthew.

My mother looked slightly less mortified. "Doesn't she live a long way from here?"

"Kempton Park. It's not that far, and Ruby has loaned me her car, so I'll be there in no time."

"And you're driving! The roads are dangerous. You must wear a scarf. I hear the smog will be bad today. And you'll get a chill if the Ghost is cold."

"Look out the window! The sun is already shining. The roads are safe, and even if the Ghost takes a knock, that thing is built like a tank, so I'll barely notice and run right over them."

"You try my nerves, you do. All this murder business is dreadful for my constitution." Mother bunched a blanket in her fist. "You must tell us everything as soon as you return home."

"If Veronica returns home." Matthew's grin was impish, while my mother grew increasingly panicked and started fretting about the smog again.

"I'm sure you don't want Todd languishing in a cell with a murder charge looming over his head," I said. "It's important we get him out as soon as possible. Now, I must go. We can't keep her ladyship waiting."

"How will you get Lady Sybil to answer questions about whether she killed Arthur?" Matthew ambled behind me into the kitchen.

"I may have suggested I'm writing a piece about Arthur for the newspaper." I collected my handbag and put on my coat.

Matthew chuckled. "How do you think she'll take it if she finds out you're not being truthful?"

"There's an element of truth to my statement. I will write Arthur's obituary."

Matthew uncharacteristically hugged me. "Watch out. And be careful on those roads. Some people have no clue how to drive."

"You know me. I'm always careful." I hugged him back. "Look after Pippin for me today."

"Of course. She's a sweet dog. She even tried to make friends with the kittens. It didn't end well. Her muzzle got scratched."

I collected Benji, said goodbye to my mother, who forced me to take three scarves and a woollen hat, and left the house. I was soon settled in Ruby's car, zooming towards Kempton Park. If I hadn't been on my way to question a murder suspect, this would have been a pleasant jolly. I enjoyed a drive in the countryside on a sunny day.

I pulled up outside the mansion half an hour later. It was even lovelier in the daylight, the grass a vibrant green and the stonework spotless.

Benji remained in the car, happy to watch the world go by with his head hanging out of the open window. Lady Sybil had made it clear at the party she wasn't dog friendly, so I wouldn't annoy her by taking him inside.

A well-mannered butler opened the front door, and escorted me into a sitting room where Lady Sybil was in residence.

She greeted me and gestured to a gold-trimmed chair with a pink cushion by the window.

"There is a lovely view from here. It's one of my favourite spots in the house."

I nodded my thanks as she passed me a delicate china cup full of strong tea and looked out the window. The view was indeed lovely, and a mild warmth filled the room as the sun lifted. The garden boasted a neat stone pathway and an assortment of colourful flowers. Tall trees offered shade, and the lawn was well kept. Farther away, a river caught my eye, its surface glistening in the sunlight. A family of swans floated lazily downstream.

"I was reluctant to permit your visit," Lady Sybil said.

"Why would that be?" I asked.

"I don't enjoy modern newspapers. They tell untruths, and they were unkind to my late husband before he passed."

"I'm sorry to hear that. I'm glad you let me visit because I consider myself a fair journalist. I always want to get to the truth."

Lady Sybil sipped from her cup. "You knew Arthur, and you seemed like a sensible woman when we met. But if I read anything disparaging about me, the party, or Arthur, ties will be cut, and I shall speak to your superior."

"I understand. My focus is writing obituaries, but I like to gather additional information that could be useful for other articles. No scandal, I assure you."

Lady Sybil drank more tea. "What do you need to know?"

I eased my notepad out and set it on my lap. "How long were you and Arthur involved?"

A small smile crossed Lady Sybil's lips. "No messing around with you, is there? My husband died eighteen months ago. I wish I could say we had a blissful marriage. We had our moments, but towards the end, it wasn't pleasant."

"He was ... unkind to you?"

"Nothing like that. But he didn't know how to enjoy himself, and I'd grown weary of his company. When he died, I appropriately mourned, but then decided to live. I needed entertainment and laughter. My late husband abhorred parties. He couldn't tolerate the noise and mess. I looked around for a suitable man, but those my own age were tiresome and long past their prime. Many of them wanted a stepmother for their children, rather than a loving companion. That wasn't for me. So, I kept searching."

"And you met Arthur?"

"I did. What a glorious specimen he was. Wonderfully handsome, funny, entertaining, and full of energy. He was exactly what I needed."

"It sounds like you were fond of him?"

"I was fond of what he brought to me. I felt as if I was fading into a grey nonexistence. Arthur brought vim and vigour to my life. Young friends, music, and dancing. It was wonderful to have such a shiny toy on my arm. I felt twenty years younger when I was with Arthur."

"A toy? That's how you describe Arthur?"

Lady Sybil laughed lightly. "I had a certain fondness for him, but the age gap meant I would never be serious with him. And now he's gone, I need a replacement."

"I imagine you do," I said cautiously.

"You may be of use to me in that regard." Lady Sybil smoothed a hand over her pretty blue dress. "Do you offer advertisements for wealthy widows looking for suitors? Discreet advertisements, of course."

I was momentarily lost for words. "It is a service we offer. Are you ready to move on so quickly?"

"Arthur was a dear heart, and I had fun with him, but much like you, I'm a sensible woman and have no time for soppiness. And I don't want to become lonely again. There's no feeling worse than loneliness. Don't you think?"

"It's never pleasant being lonely. Do you mind me asking, was Arthur content with your relationship? Did he know you referred to him as a shiny toy?"

"Arthur was excessively fond of me. He said he liked women who'd seen the world. He was utterly in love with me, and I could do no wrong in his eyes."

"That must have been lovely to meet someone like that," I said.

Lady Sybil looked at my bare ring finger. "Your time will come, my dear."

The door crashed open, and a maid came in carrying a tea tray.

"Be more careful, Alice," Lady Sybil snapped. "How many times have I told you to knock before entering a room?"

The young maid froze. "Sorry! I was sent to see if you needed more tea."

"No! Don't disturb us again. And shut the door quietly on your way out."

Alice bobbed a curtsy and dashed out, and the door thumped behind her.

Lady Sybil sighed and fussed with her cup. "It's so hard to get good staff."

"Yes. It's a struggle. When did you first hear about what happened to Arthur?" I asked.

"Alice awoke me when the police arrived the next morning," Lady Sybil said. "I hadn't gone to bed until after one in the morning, so the early alarm was unwelcome."

"It must have been a terrible shock," I said. "Especially since you and Arthur had a disagreement, and you sent him away."

Lady Sybil drew herself up to her full height. "I dislike the implication in those words, Miss Vale. Arthur left because he needed to clear his head and remember his manners. He never could handle his alcohol. I have a clear conscience. I enjoyed my party, and that was it."

"You didn't think to send someone to look for Arthur? Weren't you worried about where he'd gone?"

"He was a grown man and capable of looking after himself. How was I to know what would happen?" She stood from her seat. "Now, if you'll excuse me, I have things to do."

"My apologies if I offended you." I gathered my belongings and followed Lady Sybil to the door. "I'm just establishing the events of that evening. I'm not sure if you're aware, but the pub Arthur was found in belongs to my family."

Lady Sybil hesitated at the door, then walked back to the window and collected a discarded book. "I was not. I thought you were a journalist, not a publican."

"Both. And the Drunken Duck is a family concern." I pulled open the door and discovered Alice scuttling away. She looked over her shoulder, terror in her eyes when she realised she'd been caught listening, before she dashed around the corner and out of sight.

"Then we both want this business put to bed as soon as possible, so our reputations aren't tarnished," Lady Sybil said. "My butler will show you out. Good day."

I left the sitting room and stood in the hallway. Lady Sybil had been quick to take offence. Was it because she had a guilty conscience? And why had Alice been listening at the door?

As I explored this mystery, I was discovering more than one layer of secrets that needed unpeeling.

Chapter 11

After the butler had escorted me out of Lady Sybil's mansion, I detoured around the side of the building, on the pretense of walking Benji. Houses of this size typically had a staff entrance, which was often tucked away out of sight of the homeowner's view.

It didn't take Benji many minutes to discover a door that opened into a small, stone-floored entrance. We tucked ourselves behind a bush and watched for several minutes. Sure enough, two members of staff hurried out and into the garden, carrying tools.

I gestured for Benji to follow, then hurried to the door, and we crept inside. The small entranceway led directly into a large kitchen with a substantial workstation set in the centre. The delicious scent of fried bacon lingered, but there was only one person overseeing things. It was the maid, Alice.

I didn't want to scare her since she was standing over a frying pan that spat fat, so I gently cleared my throat.

She jumped and turned around. "Oh! Miss! Is there something I can do for you?"

"If you can spare me some time, I'd like to ask a few questions," I said, and introduced myself and Benji. "It's about the night of the party."

Alice was young, maybe twenty, with large, round blue eyes and pale skin. She looked at the main kitchen door. "Cook won't like me skipping work."

"We can talk here if you'd rather. Then you can keep an eye on things." I gestured at the bacon.

"She won't like that neither," Alice said. "If we stand just outside, then I can hear if anyone is coming."

I nodded my approval, and after a quick stir of the bacon, she hurried over, wiping her hands on a clean white cloth. "Was there a problem at the party, miss? Did you lose your handbag or shawl?"

"No, nothing like that. And please, call me Veronica," I said.

Alice shook her head. "Lady Sybil is particular about names and titles. I don't want to get in no trouble."

"You'll get no trouble from me," I said. "I'm looking into what happened after the party, though. Have you heard about Arthur Buchanan's death?"

Her eyes grew even wider.

"I assure you, I'm not looking for problems. I work at the London Times, and I was acquainted with Arthur. I'd like to know what went on that evening."

"You want quotes for a story? I shouldn't. I need to go back inside."

"Please, it'll only take a moment. You were working at the party, so you could have seen something useful."

"Not me. I'm never useful. Cook is always telling me that."

Benji nudged her hand and lifted one paw, cocking his head in a most adorable manner.

"Is your dog friendly, miss?" Alice asked. "I love dogs, but I'm not allowed one. Lady Sybil says they make too much mess and their barking gives her a headache."

"Even if they do, I expect you'd be the one clearing the mess, so it would be no matter to her. And yes, Benji is exceedingly friendly. He likes everyone with a kind heart. You can pat him if you like. He likes a good rub behind the ears."

Alice crouched and spent a good minute thoroughly scratching behind Benji's ears and all around his head, which he adored.

"He's a good boy," Alice said.

"He's the best boy. I wouldn't be without him. If you can find a way, I recommend getting your own dog."

Alice lifted one shoulder and stood. "Not while working here."

"How long have you worked for Lady Sybil?" I asked, pleased Alice was no longer so nervous.

"Six months. I lost my last position when my employer died. His widow sold up and moved to a little place by the seaside, and she had no room for staff."

"Do you enjoy your work?"

"I've had worse. I prefer working in the kitchen to serving Lady Sybil and her guests."

"I noticed Lady Sybil was sharp with you when you served the tea."

"She's scary," Alice said. "I get the shakes every time I'm around her."

"What does she do to make you scared?" I asked.

Alice tilted her head. "Scared was the wrong word, but she's firm, and I'm clumsy. I get nervous when I'm anywhere near her, and I worry about dropping things. Then the more I worry, the more likely I am to drop whatever I'm carrying. Kitchen work is better. Cook has a tongue as sharp as the carving knife, but I know where I stand with her."

"Those are your main duties?" I asked. "You help in the kitchen and serve Lady Sybil as needed?"

"I sometimes help Lady Sybil at the end of the evening. Like I did after the party."

"You're a lady's maid, too? Goodness, you have a remarkable array of talents."

Alice blushed. "Can't say much about that. It's more like needs must than I'm any good at anything."

"We all have talents. They're cultivated with hard work and determination."

"If you say so, miss."

"So, you were Lady Sybil's personal maid after the party?"

"I had no choice. Lady Sybil recently fired her maid and hasn't hired a new one. She summoned me to help her get undressed around one o'clock. She had so many buttons and ties that it took me a good ten minutes to get her out of her gown. And she had dozens of pins in her hair to keep her hairpiece secure." Alice clamped a hand over her mouth. "I shouldn't have said that. She doesn't like anyone knowing she wears hairpieces. She thinks they make her look younger. But I'm not so sure. You can see it's not real. It don't move right."

"I won't tell another soul about Lady Sybil's liking for hairpieces," I said. "What time did you leave her?"

"It must have been around thirty past one. Maybe later. I stayed up with Cook to make sure everyone had gone to bed, and we went around and put out any candles. Can't have a place like this burning to the ground."

"You and Cook work long hours," I said.

"We do. We were up at dawn on the day of the party. I was almost dead on my feet. But you never say no to Lady Sybil. She's an exacting lady and knows how things should be done. She has high standards."

"That's the impression I get of her."

Alice shuffled her feet. "I should check the bacon."

"Before you do, I wanted to ask about your relationship with Arthur." I placed a hand on Alice's arm to keep her focus on me.

A flush of colour rose up her neck, and she looked over her shoulder.

"Arthur seemed flirtatious with you at the party. Was that usual?"

"I know nothing about that, miss. Lady Sybil's gentlemen friends behave however they want. The posh lot always do."

Alice was nervous and not keen to talk about Arthur. I'd initially assumed Arthur was being overly familiar with Alice because he'd had too much to drink, but could it be more than that?

"I'm not looking for scandal," I said soothingly, treating Alice like she was a skittish, feral kitten who needed looking after. "But I want to understand what happened to Arthur. It's a terrible business, and so unfair. He was a young man in the prime of life, and someone cruelly took that life."

Alice looked down at her hands, her thumbs spinning circles around each other. "Cook said they've got the man who done it, so we've got nothing to worry about."

"The police have a number of suspects they're considering," I said. "In my role as a journalist, I work closely with them, so I have an insider scoop."

"That must be exciting work, miss," Alice said. "Although I'm not sure I'd like to poke around and ask questions about people who died."

"It has its challenges," I said. "I'm interested in Arthur's character. What can you tell me about that?"

"Nothing. I didn't know him. He was Lady Sybil's companion, not mine."

I fixed her with a stern look. "He never suggested you spend any time together? Just the two of you? As you said, the posh lot can sometimes take liberties."

"That wouldn't be right to be alone with him."

Her comment wasn't a denial. And Alice hadn't looked me in the eye since I'd stumbled upon the possibility she had more than a passing acquaintance with Arthur.

"Let's go back to the night of the party," I said. "When you served the drinks, did you see Arthur behaving oddly?"

"No. He was his usual self."

"How would you know that if you didn't know him well?"

Alice frowned. "I didn't know him well. I mean, he was around a lot, so our paths crossed, nothing else."

She was trembling, so I didn't press any harder. "What about any conversations he had with others at the party? Perhaps you overheard him arguing with someone?"

Alice jumped, and her head turned. "Did you hear a squeak? I'm sure we've got mice."

"Mice are common in country residences. After all, we built on their homes, so we must expect the occasional invasion." I glanced around the entrance way but spotted no small, furred creatures, and Benji wasn't staring at anything.

"Lady Sybil will have a fit if she discovers we have mice. And it'll be me who deals with them. I have to set the traps and deal with the bodies." Alice grimaced.

"We can help you see if you have a rodent problem," I said brightly. "Benji has an excellent nose."

"Oh! I thought it was only cats who hunted rodents." Alice peered down at Benji. "Can he really sniff them out?"

"Benji will search for anything. As you've already noted, he's a very good boy."

Benji wagged his tail in agreement.

"Could you get him to sniff around the kitchen to make sure there's nothing in there?" Alice asked. "But you need to hurry. Cook will be back any minute from the storeroom. If she finds mice in her cupboards, she'll scream the place down. She's terrible with anything like that. And I'm not much better."

"Let's not dally. I'll set Benji straight to work." I returned to the kitchen and gestured for Benji to sniff along the boards at the base of the kitchen cabinets. He did several circuits, lingering for a few seconds by the now crispy bacon still being fried.

"Shall we check the main hallway?" I asked when Benji identified no unwanted guests in the kitchen.

"Only if you're quick. I'll get in trouble if we're caught." Alice removed the bacon from the heat and set it to one side, shaking her head at the overdone contents.

I peeked into the wood-panelled hallway. There was no one there, so I hurried out with Benji, and he continued his investigation. It only took a few seconds before he stopped by a tiny hole near a closed door. He lifted his head and gave a gentle bark.

"What does that mean?" Alice was so close, she was almost stepping on my heels.

"It means, unfortunately, you may have tiny guests," I said. "Mice can squeeze through the smallest hole. You should plug that as soon as possible to discourage them. Adding cloves or peppermint to the hole will also encourage them to move on."

Alice sighed. "I keep hearing them squeak. I even heard them after the party. Squeak, squeak, squeak. Like they're talking to each other. I'd better tell Cook. She'll want me to check all the cupboards and clean them."

"Alice! What are you doing out of the kitchen?" A short, rotund woman with grey hair wearing a white apron strode towards us. That must be Cook.

"My apologies for stealing Alice," I said. "But she's been most helpful."

"Helpful? Are you a guest of Lady Sybil's?" Cook asked.

"I've just paid her a visit."

"If you've already paid your visit, shouldn't you be leaving?"

Cook was the kind of no-nonsense woman I always appreciated.

"We were just dealing with a small matter," I said. "Alice, I have two more questions."

Alice chewed on her bottom lip, then nodded.

"The night of the party, did you see Arthur leave?"

"We both did," Cook said, cutting Alice off before she'd finished taking a breath. "I helped Alice snuff out candles. That was when we heard the argument."

Alice squeaked in a most mouse-like manner.

"You didn't mention this, Alice," I said.

"And she won't, neither." Cook's tone was fearsome. "Lady Sybil detests gossip."

"Who was arguing?" I blocked the way into the kitchen, much to Cook's disgust.

"Alice, this isn't our business," Cook said. "I shouldn't have said anything."

"But you did, and I'm grateful for it. Please, I'm interested."

"They were ever so angry with each other." Alice's expression wavered between terror and excitement about sharing a secret. "I've never heard them get so angry before."

"Someone was fighting with Arthur?" I asked.

Cook sighed. "You'll get yourself in trouble if Lady Sybil overhears you."

"It was Lady Sybil arguing with Arthur?" I asked.

"It wasn't a gentle fight. And I've never heard her scream like that before. Lady Sybil was furious with Arthur," Alice said. "She shoved him out of the front door and told him not to come back."

Although I was aware there'd been a disagreement between Lady Sybil and Arthur, the argument sounded more serious than I'd been led to believe.

"That was the last we saw of Arthur," Cook said. "Now, Alice, you get back to that kitchen or you'll be in serious trouble. I expect the bacon is ruined!"

"One more question," I said.

"You've had all your questions." Cook stepped closer. "Time to leave."

I met her stern glare. "Alice, did you help a young man who'd fallen in the garden? He missed his footing on the stone steps."

"Oh! I did. Poor fella. I heard him calling for help. He was a sorry sight."

"Get in that kitchen, now!" Cook jabbed a finger at the door.

Alice finally accepted defeat and hurried into the kitchen. Cook followed Alice, shutting the door firmly.

I sneaked through the house to the front entrance, hoping I wouldn't be spotted and have to explain why I'd returned, and crept outside with Benji beside me.

Why had Lady Sybil downplayed how serious her fight with Arthur was? The lady of the house had something to hide, and I intended to find out what that was.

Chapter 12

I was hurrying to the Ghost when someone called out a greeting. Lady Sybil's uncle John wheeled himself towards me in his chair. From his determined rate of motion, he had something he wanted to talk about.

"You're Arthur's friend, aren't you?" he said as he drew nearer, a layer of dark scruff on his chin and cheeks.

I closed the gap between us and nodded. "Veronica Vale. I was visiting Lady Sybil and asking a few questions for my article in the London Times."

"John Tewksbury." His bloodshot eyes were alert as they skimmed over me. "Someone told me you were a journalist. Must be interesting work."

"It takes me to some fascinating places," I said. "Is there something I can help you with?"

"I was admiring your car. She's a beauty."

"She's fun to drive," I said. "I've borrowed her from a friend, so I need to be careful."

John moved past me and stopped by the Ghost. "I'd love a car like this to drive, but with these wheels, it puts me out of action." He moved slowly around the car, admiring its features.

"Lady Sybil is your niece, isn't she?" I followed behind him as he stopped and rubbed at a spot of dirt on the chassis.

He nodded. "My brother was her father. She ensures I'm taken care of and even lets me borrow her driver now and again. I get out and about when I want to, but it's not the same as having the freedom of your own vehicle."

"If you don't mind me asking, how long have you been in your wheelchair?"

"It's bold of you to ask. Few do. They see the chair and the failing legs and their eyes glaze because they don't know what to say."

"I've been told I can be rather forward. If you'd rather not say—"

"It doesn't bother me. I had an accident when I was a teenager. Been stuck in a chair ever since. The doctors can't fix me, and I've been to enough of them to know that's the truth." John glanced at me, an eager gleam in his eyes. "I'm not here to talk about my misfortune, or this beautiful car, though."

I'd thought as much. "What would you like to talk about?"

"Push me around the garden, and I'll tell you what I know. It could be useful for your article."

My eyebrows rose. "I'll do you one better. How about I take you for a spin in the Ghost?"

He grinned and slapped a hand on his thigh. "What a treat! You'll have to help me in. You're not exactly burly, and I don't want you putting your back out."

"I'm stronger than I look."

John chuckled. "I dare say. Once we're in the car, no one can snoop on our conversation and disapprove of me telling tales. Mind you, those tales are true."

Intrigued by his enigmatic comment, I swiftly assisted John into the passenger seat. He barely needed help and had clearly done the manoeuvre numerous times, ably swinging himself in using his arms. Once he was comfortable, I put his chair in the back and ensured it was secure, and tucked Benji in next to it, the window an inch down, so he could enjoy the fresh breeze.

"This will be a first," John said, once I was settled in the driver's seat. "I've never had a lady whizz me around the country lanes. Are you sure you know how to operate this thing?"

I speared him with a tart look. "I'm perfectly capable of operating an automobile."

He roared a laugh. "From that look, I've no doubt you're perfectly capable of doing plenty of things. Most of them fun!"

I repressed a smile and cracked open my own window, having noticed a pungent smell of alcohol coming off John. He appeared sober, although he was jovial and relaxed considering we barely knew each other.

"Head along the driveway and take a left. There's a clear straight run for a few miles. We'll do a circular route that will take us back into the village," John said.

"That sounds ideal." I glanced at him as he removed a flask from his inside jacket pocket and took a sip.

"I hope you don't mind, but it takes the edge off. I get pains in my legs."

"I have a similar flask in my handbag for emergency situations." I set off along the driveway. "What did you want to talk about?"

"Since you're asking about Arthur, I thought I could give you some background on him. I live with Sybil and spent time with Arthur when she was too busy to entertain him. His sister, too, since she's been staying. Funny old girl, but has some clever ideas."

"You saw Arthur and Lady Sybil together, too?" I navigated the narrow lane. If we met a tractor coming the other way, we'd be in a spot of bother.

"I did. I was surprised when Sybil found herself such a young man, but I didn't gossip like some about how inappropriate it was. Her husband was as much fun as a wet weekend on Herne Bay pier. I can count the number of times I heard him laugh on one hand. Sybil wanted someone who could bring fun into her world. She was never shy about stating that desire. And Arthur had fun in spades."

"She said a similar thing to me," I said. "Lady Sybil seems a practical woman, though. Not one for spontaneous affairs of the heart."

"Sybil has a heart, although she keeps it tightly locked up. She's a good sort, though. I admit to being too fond of drink and rather lazy, but Sybil lets me live here without paying a penny. I think she's taken pity on her old uncle."

"Since you're family, she'll always watch over you," I said.

"I'm glad she does, because I'm no good to anyone. I have other relatives who are far less generous."

"You may be at a disadvantage by being in that wheelchair, but I know many men who were injured during the war and who've found purpose. Some still work."

John grunted. "How can I be useful when I'm like this?"

"Does your brain function?"

"Most days."

"And your arms are strong?"

"I suppose they are."

"Then you have value. You need to find your passion. Or at least something positive and purposeful to occupy your time."

John chuckled again. "It's decent of you to say, but I'm good for nothing. I accepted that a long time ago. Even Emma said I wasn't fit to serve my country."

"Don't give in too easily," I said. "Men who have lost arms and legs or been scarred during battle go on to find meaningful employment."

"I'm too old, too sick, and too set in my ways. I'm content with my lot. Besides, I don't think I've got long left in this world. I know what I enjoy. Sybil looks after me, and most of the time, I'm free from pain."

From the amount John had drunk since settling in the car, I had to believe his time left on this earth would be limited thanks to his self-pickling liver efforts. Since Lady Sybil supported that alcohol-rich lifestyle, he would have no motivation to change.

I slowed as I squeeze the Ghost past a black Model Ford T and continued on. It was an enjoyable journey, green fields surrounding us and a fresh breeze drifting through the open windows. Benji had his tongue out, flapping in the breeze as he watched the fields whizz past.

"What did you make of Arthur's character?" I asked. "Since you spent so much time with him, you must have gotten to know him well."

"We were friendly enough. He had too much education and not enough practical experience. I've seen it before. Families over-educate their children, but they don't understand how the world works. And Arthur had funny ideas about things. Talked about social justice and equality. It had me baffled. Society works fine just the way it is. Why alter things?"

"I suspect he was finding his place in the world," I said. "The Great War disrupted everything and set people to thinking about change, so something that terrible never happens again."

John observed me for a second. "It sounds like you served."

"I did my bit."

"Funny business, allowing women to get involved in war. If I was able, I would have served. Every man should be loyal to his country and step up. Every woman, too, by the sounds of it." He eyed me some more, as if expecting me to disclose information.

I remained silent. The less I talked about serving this country, the better. It only caused unnecessary interest.

"Did Arthur and Lady Sybil ever have disagreements?" I asked.

John pulled out his flask again and grinned. "I should say they did. They had a fiery relationship."

"I heard they argued the night of the party," I said.

"I wouldn't be surprised if they did."

"You didn't hear them bicker?"

"I was otherwise engaged with a bottle of vintage port for most of the evening."

"What were their disagreements usually about?"

"I ignored the fights. I didn't want to get involved." John drained his flask and sighed, peering into the opening with one eye and frowning when he discovered it hadn't miraculously refilled itself. "I know Sybil didn't like Arthur going out without her. It was one of the reasons she had so many parties at the house."

"You don't think she trusted Arthur?"

"Why would she? Sybil was with Arthur because he made her look good when she was out. Older woman, younger man. It was the talk of the town."

"Lady Sybil told you that?"

"Arthur did. We'd had a lot to drink one night, and he was talking about whether he'd done the right thing by attaching his wagon to Sybil. I asked what he meant, and he said he'd overheard her friends talking about wanting a younger model themselves and how lucky Sybil was to have snagged him. He was embarrassed."

"Did Arthur confess his love for Lady Sybil?"

"Love! Their relationship wasn't about love. And Sybil knew it. She got to have fun and be the envy of her friends, and Arthur got to roll about in her money. They were both winners."

I arched an eyebrow. That wasn't what Lady Sybil had told me. She'd seemed assured when she said Arthur adored her and had no interest in her cash. Who was telling the truth?

"When was the last time you saw Arthur alive?" I asked.

John thought for a moment. "It wasn't long before I was sent to bed."

"Excuse me? Someone sent you to bed?"

He laughed again and sank back into the seat. "Arthur's sullen sister, Emma, did you meet her? Anyway, she told me off because I'd had too much to drink and kept running over people's toes. I remember I bashed into your pretty friend."

"You did. Ruby got an abrupt introduction when you hit her," I said.

"I hope she didn't get bruised. I lose control of my wheels when I'm under the influence. The police should take my chair away for reckless driving." That idea set him to laughing again.

"Ruby is made of stern stuff. And she's usually covered in bruises."

"Why would that be?"

"Part of her job involves riding horses," I said. "They can get feisty."

"You ladies are extraordinary. Driving cars, dealing with difficult horses, writing newspaper articles. Remarkable."

"That's kind of you to say. We have many talents." I returned to my question. "Do you remember what time it was when you last saw Arthur?"

"It was getting late. Arthur was worse for wear and stumbling about. Sybil was looking annoyed, so I assumed a fight was on the cards. I was helping myself to more port when someone jerked on the handles of my chair. I looked around and it was Emma! She told me I was setting a bad example for the younger people." John tipped back his head and chortled. "How they behaved had nothing to do with me! But Emma wouldn't listen, and she wouldn't let go of my chair, no matter how much I argued. Stubborn old thing. She took me to my bedroom, which is on the ground floor, and insisted I stay there."

"Did you stay?"

"I had no choice. Emma stood by the door until I got out of the chair and sat on the bed. Then she took my wheels to the farthest corner of the room so it was hard to reach. I wasn't happy, but she said I'd had too much to drink, and was making a fool of myself. She's no fun, that one."

"It sounds like you were a prisoner in your own room," I said.

"I could have gotten to my chair, and I intended to, but once Emma turned out the light and left the room, I passed out. I woke fully clothed when someone knocked on my door and told me what happened to Arthur."

By now, we'd done a half circle and were in the village, passing the post office, general store, and pond.

"John, what do you think happened to Arthur at the pub?" I asked.

He went quiet, his gaze looking out over the pond. "Have you spoken to his friend Peter Appleby? He was at the party."

"No, but I have plans to."

"They were close. Peter works in the city. He has a place in London, and Arthur was always spending time with him. He'd go to London for the day and end up sleeping at Peter's, and return the next morning with a sore head and plenty of tales, much to Sybil's disapproval."

"Did you see something happen at the party that caused you concern about Peter?"

John nodded. "They were playing billiards together and got into an argument. Peter accused Arthur of cheating, and he wanted his money back. I guess they were placing wagers on who won."

"Arthur didn't like being accused of cheating?"

"He tried to hit Peter with a cue and chased him around the table. Peter had to jump out of a window to get away from him."

"This is the first I'm hearing about the fight."

"It happened so quickly, most of the guests missed it. I suppose I got lucky. When I saw Peter later that evening, he didn't look happy. I don't think those two spoke for the rest of the night."

"Where did Peter go after the party ended?" I asked. "Could he have come into the village?"

"I couldn't tell you. I was dead to the world."

I slowed as we reached the Drunken Duck pub. Perhaps Peter had come here. He wanted to finish his argument with Arthur, and things got out of hand.

"I'm in the mood for an early snifter," John said. "Park up and let me out."

"Bridget won't be open at this time." I pulled over, anyway.

"You know the landlady?"

I nodded. "Very well."

"So do I." John grinned. "And she always lets me in, whatever time it is. My custom is valued. Or should I say, Sybil's money is valued."

I'd have to speak to Bridget about opening outside of regular hours. "How will you get home?"

"I'll telephone Sybil's driver. Bridget keeps the number behind the bar. Hurry! All this talking has got me parched."

I got John's wheelchair out of the back of the car and helped him into it.

"I hope I've been useful," he said. "It's a shame what happened to Arthur. I expect I'll hear the latest from Bridget, though. She loves to share everyone's secrets over a pint of ale."

"Yes, she's always helpful," I murmured. "As are you. Our conversation has been more useful than you realise."

Chapter 13

The evening was chilly. Too chilly to remain on the steps outside the police station waiting for Ruby a second longer. She was fifteen minutes late as I admitted defeat and stepped through the doorway.

Following my meeting with Lady Sybil and the impromptu and most productive drive through the countryside with John, I'd returned to work and focused on writing obituaries for a retired music teacher, a young chap who had an unfortunate incident with an open-topped bus, and a man who had a disagreement with the River Thames. The river won.

I was eager to update Ruby on my discoveries and see how Todd was faring. The police couldn't hold him for much longer. If they didn't have enough evidence to charge him, they had to let him go.

I strode to the desk, introduced myself, and asked to speak to Inspector Templeton. I was told to wait, although this time, I chose not to sit in an uncomfortable chair. Instead, I slowly paced with Benji beside me, rubbing my hands together to get warmth back into them.

Inspector Templeton finally appeared, looking careworn and grumpy. "Veronica. Always a treat."

"There's no need to be snippy. Have you not had time for dinner yet?"

"Is that an invitation?"

I patted my pocket. "If you're desperate, I could rustle up a dog chew."

He smirked, then held out his hand for Benji.

"You know why I'm here," I said.

"The more you make a nuisance of yourself and waste my time, the longer this investigation will take."

"Gathering information to ensure an innocent man isn't sent down for a crime he didn't commit is nobody's waste of time," I said. "Have you performed an autopsy on Arthur?"

"I... My skills don't stretch to conducting autopsies."

Irritating man. "You know very well what I mean. Since the cause of death wasn't clear when his body was discovered, your people must be conducting tests."

"We are."

"And?"

Inspector Templeton pressed his lips together and shook his head.

The door behind me burst open, and Ruby dashed in, looking red-faced and wearing straw-covered jodhpurs. "Sorry! I had to visit Lady M. She telephoned and said there was an emergency. Although her definition of an emergency beggars belief! She'd lost her reading glasses, mistook the gardener as a burglar, and a horse had gotten loose. I said I could stay for an hour, but when I tried to leave, she refused to let me go."

"Lady M knows you have a family emergency to deal with, though," I said.

"She does! Of course, I couldn't tell her Todd was up on a murder charge in case she thought I was tainted too, so I've downplayed the situation. The beastly woman wouldn't let me leave until I'd found her glasses, confirmed the gardener wasn't interested in stealing her jewels or furs, and the horse was back in his stable."

"I'm glad you got everything sorted for her," I said.

"At great personal cost." Ruby shook straw off her thigh. "Inspector, where can I stable my horse?"

His mouth dropped open, and his brow lowered. "Your... horse?"

"Yes! Riding here was the quickest option. I considered a taxi, but at this time of the evening, the roads are clogged. My lovely boy is tied up outside, but I don't want to leave him for long."

A bubble of laughter came out of me and it wouldn't stop, growing louder as Inspector Templeton grew more furious with Ruby.

"You can't ride a horse on the busy streets of London," he said. "You could have had an accident. You most likely caused some, since the sight of a woman astride a horse in the centre of London is an uncommon sight."

"Horse and carriages were once commonly used," Ruby said. "I remember them being a thoroughly normal sight on the roads. It's only recently we've become comfortable with open-topped buses, cars, and taxis."

"That still doesn't make your behaviour right," Inspector Templeton said.

"You have mounted policemen." There wasn't the hint of an apology in Ruby's voice. "They must stable their horses close by. I'm sure one of them will secure a temporary place for my boy. Unless you want the poor creature to leave a mess outside."

I had to look away as Inspector Templeton huffed and puffed and scolded Ruby before giving in.

"I'm not happy about this." He left us in the reception area, his stomping feet a declaration of his foul mood.

"Goodness me! The way he's complaining, you'd think I'd flown in astride a twin-engine Gotha. It's just a horse. A very nice one at that." Ruby blinked in surprised innocence.

I plucked more straw off her jodhpurs. "I was worrying about you. And I've got news."

"Do you know who killed Arthur?"

"No, but I have new suspects and information you'll want to hear. My visit to Lady Sybil's was informative."

"Then the quicker I get the horse dealt with, the better. Where is your Inspector Templeton? He'd better not take his bad mood out on Todd. How was I to know he didn't like horses?"

"He likes them well enough, but I suspect Inspector Templeton doesn't like horses illegally parked outside the station." That thought made me laugh again.

He returned a moment later, with a tall, lean man who had a mildly surprised look on his face as he learned there was a horse stationed outside, but he was happy to escort Ruby and the horse to the mounted police officers' stables.

Inspector Templeton didn't wait with me and attempt friendly small talk, and for that, I was grateful. I was still chuckling over his reaction to Ruby's mode of transport, and that would only have increased his frustration.

When Ruby returned, minus the horse, Inspector Templeton escorted us to the interview room where Todd was waiting.

Todd jumped up and held out his hand to me. "Thanks for sorting the business with our solicitor. I feel terrible about you paying our debts. I'll get the money to you as soon as I can."

"Think nothing of it." I warmly shook his hand. "We need to make sure we have the best people looking after you."

"Are they still feeding you?" Ruby pressed a kiss to her brother's cheek.

"They're looking after me," Todd said. "I had a decent sandwich at lunchtime."

"I doubt that very much." Ruby slid a glare at Inspector Templeton as she sat in a seat. "Veronica's been busy gathering suspects."

"Has she now?" Inspector Templeton took the chair next to me. "I'll be most interested in what she's learned."

"I'm sure you will," I said. "Because you have the wrong man for Arthur's murder. But before I begin, you were about to tell me about the results of Arthur's autopsy."

"I don't recall that I was," Inspector Templeton said.

"However Arthur died, it had nothing to do with me," Todd said. "I have been thinking, though."

"Go on. Do you have a confession to make?" Inspector Templeton asked.

Ruby tutted, and I affixed him with a fierce glower.

"No!" Todd said. "But I will confess the fight I had with Arthur was more serious than I originally told you."

"Witnesses at the party saw you exchange blows," Inspector Templeton said. "So I was aware you weren't being truthful."

Todd ducked his head in shame. "I was embarrassed. Arthur was a good friend, and it should never have gone that far. We'd been drinking, and I was overexcited. Then I got angry with him and said things I shouldn't. My last words to Arthur were spiteful, and there's no way to make up for that now he's gone."

"What was your argument about?" I asked.

Todd sighed. "I had an idea for a new business, but I needed an investor. Arthur had his connection to Lady Sybil, so I figured he'd be good for a loan."

"Arthur refused to give you the money?"

"Veronica, I'm in charge of this investigation," Inspector Templeton said.

"I'm simply asking the same questions you would," I said. "Save your voice. It's already hoarse with tiredness."

"The less about horses, the better. Go ahead, Todd. It was a fight about money?" Inspector Templeton asked.

Todd nodded. "He wouldn't give me a penny. He said I couldn't be relied upon, and that everyone knew the problems our family was having. I was humiliated. Arthur was supposed to be a friend, but he left me in the lurch."

"This information gives you an excellent motive for killing him," Inspector Templeton said.

"Then we've arrived at opposite conclusions," I said. "With Arthur dead, Todd has no way of convincing Arthur to give him a loan."

"Exactly! I figured I'd be able to talk Arthur around," Todd said. "Now he's gone, that won't be possible."

"It leaves your way clear to Lady Sybil," Inspector Templeton said. "Perhaps you thought you could take Arthur's place and become her new favourite. Get the money that way."

Todd looked appalled. "I would never ask a woman for money. I have standards."

"Didn't I overhear you thanking Veronica because she paid a debt for you?" Inspector Templeton asked.

"That was different! I didn't know Veronica would do that, and I will pay her back."

"There's no rush," I said. "You need your solicitor here to advise you."

Ruby glanced at Inspector Templeton, narrowing her eyes, then focused on Todd. "We haven't had things easy recently. I'm not surprised Arthur thought you were a risk."

Todd glowered at her. "You're supposed to be helping. Why isn't anybody helping me?"

"Who else is causing you trouble?" I asked.

Todd shifted in his seat. "Even though you paid Basil's debt, when he visited to review my case, he was no use. When I told him my alibi, or rather my lack of it, he shuffled papers around in his briefcase and said he'd see what he could do. By the time we'd finished talking, I felt guilty."

"I've never thought much of that man," Ruby said. "He's well past retirement age. We should find someone else to represent you."

"I can speak to Basil for you," I said. "Present him with the evidence I've gathered. That may inspire him to become more useful."

"You should share that evidence with us," Inspector Templeton said. "It seems my highly trained team of experts have missed valuable clues."

I arched a brow. "I'd be happy to. I visited Lady Sybil this morning. I learned more about her character and her feelings for Arthur. Or rather, her lack of them."

"Arthur was getting embarrassed about their situation," Todd said. "He was thinking about ending things with Lady Sybil."

"There's a better motive!" Ruby exclaimed. "Arthur wanted out of the relationship, but Lady Sybil wouldn't let him go."

"I've spoken to Lady Sybil," Inspector Templeton said. "She provided me with an alibi, and I have no doubts about it. She didn't kill Arthur."

"I spoke to her maid, Alice. She helped Lady Sybil get to bed that night, but it's possible she crept out when no one was around. She'll know the quiet routes and shortcuts like the back of her hand, since she has lived there for so long."

Ruby bounced in her seat. "What's to say Lady Sybil didn't sneak into the village and do away with Arthur?"

"Because she is a lady with an excellent character," Inspector Templeton said. "Why kill Arthur when she could have found another chap? Her situation is appealing to many."

I didn't like his logical path, so diverted to another possibility. "My conversation with Alice was interesting.

Do you know if she was involved with Arthur?" I asked Todd.

Todd's forehead furrowed. "Not that I know of. The man was an incorrigible flirt, though. He could have said a few things to the maid and given her the wrong idea."

"If they were involved, he'd have needed to keep it a secret," Ruby said. "If word got back to Lady Sybil he was carrying on with a maid behind her back, she wouldn't have been happy."

"I suppose so," Todd said. "But I saw nothing that made me suspicious. And he never could keep a secret, so I'd have known if something was going on."

"We've spoken to the household staff," Inspector Templeton said. "No one mentioned any relationship between Arthur and Alice."

"Because they were keeping it a secret!" Ruby said.

"Alice was certainly nervous," I said. "She would be worth speaking to again."

"I'll make a note of it," Inspector Templeton said. "Have you added anyone else to your suspect list, or am I free to do my job?"

I adjusted my skirt hem and smoothed it with a hand. "Two more people."

He sighed. "If I'd known we'd be this long, I'd have brought in tea."

"How thoughtful, but please don't trouble yourself. I spoke to Lady Sybil's uncle. John is an interesting character. He told me about the dreadful fights Lady Sybil and Arthur got into. Their relationship was fiery," I said.

"Another black mark against Lady Sybil," Ruby said.

"John was the chap in the wheelchair, wasn't he?" Todd asked.

"That's right. Lady Sybil has taken him in. He made me wonder about Arthur's friend, Peter. Todd, do you know much about him?"

"We often spend time together. He's jolly good fun. Works in the city, and always has plenty of money to throw around. Bit of a show-off, but his heart is in the right place. Don't peg him as a killer."

"John said he saw Arthur and Peter arguing during a game of billiards. There was an accusation of cheating, and Arthur got angry. He chased Peter until he fled out of a window."

Todd chuckled. "I would have enjoyed seeing that."

"I've yet to speak to Peter," I said, "but if he has a temper, he could have gotten revenge on Arthur. He could have followed him to the pub and attacked him."

"This is wild guesswork. You don't have a shred of evidence to support that claim," Inspector Templeton said. "Peter Appleby's background has been checked. He has no criminal convictions and an excellent job in the city. He would lose that if he was involved in a murder."

Todd also looked unconvinced. "Peter can be full of himself, but he's not malicious. He's a good-time guy who enjoys a fun night out with the ladies and hard work. I can't imagine he'd kill Arthur because they argued over who cheated during a game of billiards."

"He's another suspect," I said bluntly. "Inspector Templeton, you may have checked his character, but do you have his alibi?"

A furious glow lit his cheeks. "I'm sure I have, but I'll have to check my notes."

I laid my hands flat on the table. "Excellent. That's quite enough for you to be getting on with."

"Excuse me?" Inspector Templeton jerked back in his chair as if a Pekinese pup had nipped his hand.

His frosty tone didn't make me cower. "I only had to spend a morning doing a brief bit of digging, and I discovered several suspects for you to follow up on. Suspects who have dubious alibis and motives for wanting Arthur dead. Why aren't they all locked up under suspicion of murder, just like Todd?"

"Because they didn't conceal a serious fight with the victim that occurred a few hours before he was later found dead."

"Lady Sybil did," Ruby said. "But then you consider her a lady of outstanding character. Perhaps *you* have a mind to fill the space Arthur left. You are still single, aren't you? And the age difference isn't so great."

"That's quite enough of that." Inspector Templeton looked ready to evict Ruby from the police station again. "I will forgive your lack of manners due to the stress of this situation, but I will not be disrespected. If you continue with that tone, I'll prevent you from visiting your brother."

"You absolute stinker! Don't you dare." Ruby grabbed my arm. "Don't let him. Veronica, tell him he can't do that."

I stood in an effort to break the tension. "I'm sure I don't have to tell you this, inspector, but you have no firm evidence or a confession to show Todd is the killer.

While you continue to investigate, you should release him."

No one took a breath as they waited for Inspector Templeton to respond. Even Benji stopped wagging his tail and lifted a paw.

Inspector Templeton pushed back his chair and stood, towering over me. "Very well. Todd, you're free to go."

I hadn't expected him to roll over so easily. "You're releasing him without charge?"

"For now. But stay close, Todd Smythe. I'm not done with you. None of you!"

Chapter 14

"This is the perfect way to celebrate my release." Todd popped a plump chip into his mouth.

We'd stopped at the fish and chip shop on Monmouth Street on the way to my house and ordered large portions of cod and chips to take home and share with my mother and Matthew. Mother had even gotten out of bed to join us around the large, well-worn wooden kitchen table to hear the latest news.

"I'm so glad you're free," she said to Todd. "I admire Inspector Templeton, but he made a mistake arresting you. Everyone knows you're a good fellow."

"Thanks, Mrs Vale." Todd fed a piece of fish to Pippin, who sat by his side, an adoring look in her eyes, happy they were reunited.

"I knew Veronica would set things right," my mother said. "Of course, she shreds my nerves to pieces poking around in business which is no concern of hers. But I understand why she had to help."

"We're not out of the woods yet," I said. "Inspector Templeton released Todd because he doesn't have enough evidence to charge him with murder, but I fear Todd is still at the top of his suspect list."

"The way Inspector Templeton glowered and griped at us when we left, he thinks we're all guilty of something." Ruby munched on a chunk of crispy fish batter.

"He can't think Todd is guilty. Not after all the suspect names you gave him." My mother shook her head.

I'd updated Matthew and her as soon as we'd arrived home, so she was up to speed with the latest suspect list.

"The way Inspector Templeton was being so shifty about the autopsy results, I can only imagine the outcome hasn't helped him secure a conviction." Ruby was settled beside her brother, glancing at him with fond exasperation.

"I should have been more forceful," I said. "How can I be useful to Inspector Templeton if we don't have all the information?"

"He's too proud," Ruby said. "If you solve another case for him, he'll look incompetent."

"Inspector Templeton doesn't strike me as an old-fashioned sort," Todd said. "Some men take umbrage when a woman offers assistance, but he seems sensible."

"He has moments of sense," I said. "In truth, he is a decent detective, but his stubborn-headed nature gets in the way. He becomes fixed on a suspect and fails to look past them. And that's been to your detriment."

"He'll get to the right conclusion," my mother said. "Once you two are friendly again, you'll have to invite him around for dinner."

I groaned inwardly and ate more delicious chips.

As my family discussed the whys and wherefores of the murder, and how to ensure Todd's innocence, he leaned in close. "I hate to ask, but would you mind keeping Pippin for now, just in case."

"In case of what?" I whispered.

"As you said, Inspector Templeton has got his sights set on me. If he finds something incriminating, I'll be a goner."

"Will he find anything incriminating?"

"No! No! I just worry about Pippin. I may have to go in for more questioning and get stuck at the police station for hours. I don't want Pippin left home alone. She likes company."

"I'm happy to keep her here. Benji is fond of her, and she's no trouble," I said.

"That's a relief. Thanks, Veronica."

I continued to eat my fish, but I was unable to dispel a flicker of worry batting at my insides like a kitten with a felt mouse. If Todd was innocent, why did he want me to keep Pippin? Was he afraid evidence he concealed would come to light that proved he'd been involved with Arthur's murder? I didn't like that possibility one bit, but I had to keep an open mind. Sometimes, behind the sweetest smiles, were the darkest souls.

"All I care about is that you're free." Ruby kissed Todd's cheek. "And I'll fight Inspector Templeton with my bare fists if he attempts to slap the cuffs on you again."

"To stop him doing that, we need to find the killer," I said. "I've questioned Lady Sybil, Alice, and John Tewksbury, but I must talk to Peter Appleby as soon as possible."

"I can help with that task," Todd said. "How about I fix up something for tomorrow evening?"

"Excellent. It would be good to get this solved." I leaned behind Todd and poked Ruby in the arm. "Haven't you forgotten something?"

She looked around the table. "I don't think so. I added salt and vinegar."

"Your horse? He's still at the police stables."

Ruby shrieked, leapt to her feet, and dashed out of the room, our laughter following her.

"What's this about a horse?" my mother asked.

I smiled. "I'll tell you everything."

I closed my file on the obituary about the retired teacher who'd had a troubling case of gout, tidied my desk, then headed into my uncle's office.

"Close the door, Veronica," he said, not looking up from the copy he was checking.

This was an unusual request, but I obliged before taking a seat. "Is something wrong?"

Uncle Harry leaned back in his seat and linked his fingers behind his head. "Bob's been complaining about you again."

"Complaining about me is his latest hobby. I'm hoping he'll move on to something more fascinating, like darts or a pub quiz. Perhaps I should offer some suggestions."

Uncle Harry narrowed his eyes. "You know why he's unhappy. You need to keep your head down."

"I'm doing my best, but when a friend is accused of murder, I won't sit back and allow an injustice to happen."

"That's an admirable trait, but you're making waves. Waves I don't have time to navigate," Uncle Harry said.

"What do you suggest I do? Simply by being here, I annoy Bob."

"I've given you some respite by making him lead reporter on a juicy fraud case. He has days of research and interviews to get through, but it won't be long before he's back to hounding me about you."

"Thank you, Uncle Harry. I'll do my best to stay out of his way, but Bob is so easy to aggravate. And sometimes, he deserves it. He has a cave man's attitude towards women. The war showed everyone what we're capable of, and I'm not living small because it upsets his grubby apple cart."

"I won't argue with you on that point." Uncle Harry stared at me with calm, intelligent eyes. "I hope you're staying safe while looking into this murder."

His concern warmed me. "Always. But I must be off. I'm catching up with Todd, Ruby, and one of his friends."

Uncle Harry sighed. "You won't leave the murder investigation alone, will you?"

"I assure you, once Todd's name is cleared, I'll focus solely on my obituaries."

"How long will that last?"

I stood and headed to the door. "As long as justice continues to be served. I'll see you tomorrow."

I left the office and headed into the damp evening with Benji. We walked for half an hour, and then I hailed a taxi to take us the rest of the way to the Smythe family home. Ruby and Todd's parents lived in a rambling, detached cottage in Wood Green. Although Ruby preferred a room closer to her work, Todd had stayed in the family home and moved into private lodgings in the garden.

Todd had suggested to Peter we get-together this evening to reminisce about Arthur and raise a drink or two in his name. Peter had been happy with the proposition, which left me with concerns. If he was guilty, he'd keep far away from this situation for fear the finger of blame shifted to him. Although, maybe he was excellent at deception. Ruby had said his character changed, so he could be hiding his true self behind a mask of sorrow.

The taxi dropped us off, and I paid the fare and climbed out with Benji. I was ten minutes early, so walked around the main family home. I was sad to see there were several roof tiles missing, and a windowpane had been broken and was yet to be fixed. The garden was also running wild with weeds and long grass. Ruby had told me her parents had let their gardener go and were struggling to stay on top of things. I dearly hoped their work in Scotland gave them the resources they needed to be more comfortable.

I led Benji farther into the garden, and he was content to bound around, jumping into the long grass and wagging his tail. He was never happier than when exploring.

It was good to get away from the hustle and bustle of London life. Wood Green was much quieter and more peaceful. I enjoyed the convenience of being in the city, but my mother was right. The air tasted different when you got away from the busy roads and crowds.

I rounded the corner and saw Todd's lodgings. There were no lights on, so I returned to the house, thinking he was using the main family residence for our get-together, since there would be more room.

I checked the time and knocked on the door. No one answered, so I did another circuit around the building, looking for a light. It was quiet. If Todd was inside, he hadn't heard me knock.

Benji's ears pricked, his tail stiffened, and he bounded away.

"Benji! No rabbit chasing," I called out. "I don't want you covered in mud and grass stains."

Although Benji enjoyed dashing after the wildlife, he never injured what he chased. He was as soft-hearted as me, and when a new foster arrived, he was always by its side, making sure it wasn't scared or in pain, and showing off the best spots for snoozing.

I lost sight of him for a few minutes and ended up striding in the long grass, calling his name. It was unlike Benji to ignore me. I turned the corner, bringing me back to Todd's lodgings. Benji was standing outside the door.

I hurried over. Benji looked at me and whined.

"What's the matter, boy? You've been here plenty of times. Worried Todd has forgotten your treats?"

There was a thump from inside, something smashed, and a man yelped.

"Todd! Is everything okay? Are you hurt?" I rushed to the door. It was slightly open.

Before I could investigate further, a figure blasted out, slammed into me, and sent me flying. I lost my balance in a flurry of surprise and shock and staggered back.

Benji was barking, and the world was a blur. Whoever fled Todd's home wasn't a welcome visitor.

I regained my composure and dashed after the villain, sprinting to catch whoever it was. I rounded the corner of the lodgings just as a tree branch swung at my head. The last thing I heard before the world turned to black was a sickening thump.

Chapter 15

Something damp was pressed against my nose. I tried to move my head, but regretted it as a blaze of pain rocketed across my forehead. The dampness returned, and my irritation grew. What was going on?

I inched open my eyes and discovered Benji had his muzzle pressed on my face, his nose against mine. He lay full length across my body, so I was pinned to the ground.

He whimpered when I blinked, and lifted his head to briefly lick my chin before pressing his paws hard against my shoulders, as if to say: *don't move. I have everything under control. No one will hurt you now I'm here.*

I was glad Benji was guarding me because I was at a loss as to what had happened. I was walking Benji. He ran off, and I discovered him outside Todd's lodgings. The door was open, and...

"There was an attacker," I whispered. "Someone ran out, and we chased them."

Benji whimpered again, as if to confirm my words.

I remembered the branch swinging towards me. I should have been more careful, but I'd been so surprised, I'd not had my rational head on. And look where that had gotten me. Running after danger was not a smart move.

Benji lifted his head and growled softly, causing me to tense. Benji never growled without reason. Was my attacker returning to finish the job? Or had he returned for Todd? I needed to ensure Todd wasn't hurt. I recalled hearing a yelp from inside his lodgings so he could be injured, too.

Benji growled again but refused to move off me, so I couldn't turn my head to assess the situation. A second later, I heard voices drawing closer. Benji stopped growling. He climbed off me and stood alert. Then he issued two loud barks.

"That was Benji!" Ruby said, her voice sounding distant. "Where are you, boy?"

I was never more grateful to hear her. A quiet male voice accompanied hers, but I didn't recognise it. It was safe to assume it was Peter, though.

"Follow Benji's bark." Speaking sent a ricochet of pain through my head, but I had to let her know where I was, and I needed help.

"Veronica and Benji can walk for hours. I can never keep up with them. I trot beside them like an over-excited horse, and then I get a stitch and end up complaining. Not that I'm a natural complainer," Ruby said.

The man said something else, and Ruby laughed. It was the laugh she used when charmed by a man. Did she never learn?

"I'm more for reclining on a chaise lounge than gallivanting around muddy fields. Unless I'm on horseback. Oh! Veronica, whatever's happened?" She was suddenly beside me, grabbing my hand. "Your head!"

"Don't worry about me. You need to see to Todd."

"Todd? I don't understand."

"Did he do this to you?" Peter Appleby appeared in my vision, concern in his gaze.

"No. Someone was attacking Todd when I arrived. I disturbed them and gave chase," I said.

"Veronica! If you intend to chase the bad guys, you must have me by your side," Ruby said.

"I'm fine," I murmured. "It's just a bruise."

"A bruise! You have a large cut on your forehead," Ruby said. "It's almost leaked down to your eyebrow. You're lucky you didn't get blood on your clothes. It's almost impossible to get out of some fabrics."

"I'm bleeding?" I gingerly reached up and touched something warm and damp on my skin.

"Peter, go inside and check on Todd. I'll stay with Veronica to ensure she does nothing foolish," Ruby said.

"Righto. Be back in a minute." He dashed away.

"Are you sure someone was after Todd?"

I blinked twice to confirm, since the world spun and there were two of Ruby and Benji every time I spoke.

"Who would attack my brother?" Ruby asked. "How did they even know the police had sent him home?"

"Someone had it in for him," I whispered. "Help me up."

"Stay down. You could have a concussion."

"I'll feel better upright. And Benji was being an excellent nurse before you arrived. I already feel almost as good as new." If only things would stop moving and my stomach would settle. And as for the thumping headache... best not to dwell on that. It only made things worse.

Benji stood an inch from my side, his gaze intent on me.

"It's fortunate Benji wasn't hurt, too. He'd do anything to protect you." Ruby briefly patted him.

I lifted a hand and wriggled my fingers.

She sighed, then grasped my hand gently and eased me to my feet. The world spun again, and I considered kneeling in the dirt until things calmed down, but I had to know what was going on with Todd.

Ruby brushed dirt off my clothing and inspected the head wound. "It's not too deep, although your skin is grey and you're swaying as if you've had too many strong gins at the club. Hold on to me. I'll get you inside, then I'll find somewhere for you to sit and rustle up some tea. Or would you prefer a brandy? Todd always has brandy in, although he hides it from me."

"I'll be fine. Stop fussing and find me that seat," I said. "Then see how Todd is. You must be worried about him."

"He has a head twice as thick as yours, so I'm sure no harm was done. At least, nothing that can't be fixed." Ruby inched us through the open door and into the kitchen, nudging me into a chair beside Todd's tiny wooden table. "I'll take a quick peek. Benji, stay with Veronica. Bark if she does anything reckless."

"He's not going anywhere." I rested a hand on my faithful dog's head.

After one more worried look at me, Ruby hurried out of the kitchen.

I closed my eyes and took several long, deep breaths. That had been a close call. If the attacker had been any stronger, I wouldn't be sitting in this chair.

Ruby rushed back into the kitchen, relief on her face. "Todd is fine. Shocked and worried about you, but not seriously hurt."

"He sustained an injury?" I accepted the glass of water Ruby poured for me and sipped on it, my hand shaking, and allowed her to clean my head wound.

"Once I've tidied you up, you can see for yourself. He's playing the walking wounded in his bedroom. Or rather, the reclining wounded. He's so dramatic."

Five minutes later, and after gathering my strength, with the help of Ruby's arm around my waist and Benji leaning against my leg, I made my way slowly to Todd's bedroom. It was small, just like the other rooms, and had the messy air of a bachelor with no young lady to take him in hand. The furnishings were sparse but clean. Todd lay on a single bed, propped up on several pillows.

"Veronica! I heard what happened to you," he said. "We have matching bumps. Although mine is on the back of my head."

"I should telephone the police and let them know what's going on." Peter was perched on the end of Todd's bed, but had stood when we entered.

"I don't have a telephone." Todd fished keys out of his trouser pocket. "Go to the main house, and you'll find one in the hallway."

Peter took the keys and dashed away.

Ruby insisted I sit on the end of Todd's bed, then settled herself beside me. "Why would you let someone inside when they wanted to attack you?" she asked her brother.

"I did nothing of the sort!" Todd winced and lowered his voice. "I knew you were all visiting, so I unlocked the front door. I was getting a few things ready when I heard it open and assumed it was one of you."

"Didn't you think it was odd when we didn't announce ourselves?" I asked.

"Not really. Ruby is always sneaking in and poking around when she shouldn't," Todd said.

"I do not poke or sneak!"

"You always steal my brandy and biscuits without asking," Todd said. "Anyway, I wasn't worried. I have no enemies. When I didn't receive a reply, I thought nothing of it. I was preparing drinks, then went into the living room to greet my guest."

"That's where you found the man who attacked you?" Ruby asked.

"No, there was no one there. I called out a greeting. Then I told you, Ruby, to stop messing around." Todd raised his eyebrows as he looked at me. "She likes to hide and jump out on me."

"You make me sound like an absolute terror," Ruby said.

I smiled despite my aching head. "Where did you find your attacker?"

"They must have hidden in the cupboard under the stairs," Todd said. "I was walking to my bedroom when I heard a creak. That's when I got a whack on the back of the head. I slammed into the floor and must have passed out for a few seconds."

"How frightening." Ruby reached over and squeezed Todd's arm. "I shall never jump out at you again."

He chuckled. "You're terrible at hiding. I always hear your heels tapping on the floorboards, so I know where you are. I just pretend I don't. Anyway, whoever whacked me turned me over to see if they'd done enough damage. The movement woke me, and I grabbed them."

"Did you tussle?" Ruby asked.

"No, but they were startled. They struggled out of my grip and ran. That was when you met them, Veronica."

"Whoever it was, they were in a hurry to leave," I said. "They almost knocked me over because they were going so fast. Did you see who it was?"

Todd carefully shook his head. "Their face was covered. Some sort of black mask."

"From the brief glimpse I got, that's what I saw, too," I said. "Whoever it was, they were taller than me. I remember that much."

"Not as tall as me," Todd said. "Not muscular, either. When I came to, I grabbed an arm. It was more plump flesh than muscular bicep."

"What about the colour of the eyes?" Ruby asked. "They couldn't have those covered, too, or they wouldn't have been able to see."

"I'm unsure," Todd said. "Veronica?"

"I can't say for certain."

Todd touched the back of his head and grimaced. "They can't have broken in thinking they'd find anything of value."

"If they were looking for loot, they'd have gone to the main house first. Although an unlocked door would be a temptation for many," I said.

"You must have done someone wrong," Ruby said. "Have you been making enemies recently?"

"You know I don't make enemies. I want to be friends with everyone."

Peter returned and entered the bedroom. "I've contacted the police. They're sending someone straight away."

"Do you know who they're sending?" I asked.

"When I told them who'd been attacked, they put me through to Inspector Jacob Templeton. Do you know him?"

"In a way." I was almost grateful he'd be attending the crime scene. Inspector Templeton was terse, but he was a thoroughly decent man to have on your side when the chips were down.

"I'll make tea for everyone, shall I?" Peter asked.

"That would be super," Ruby said. "I'll stay here and look after the wounded. And dig out Todd's brandy. It's in the top middle cupboard behind the empty biscuit tin."

"How the devil do you know that?" Todd scowled at Ruby. "Such a little snoop."

"There's no need to make a fuss. I'm barely wounded," I said. "I'll help with the tea."

"Your colour has improved a fraction," Ruby said. "But I'm not taking my eyes off of you. Neither is Benji. Remain on the bed. That's an order. Peter is in charge of refreshments."

"What about me?" Todd asked. "You must make sure I don't have a sudden relapse."

"A relapse from what? You're snuggled in a comfortable bed with a tiny bump on your noggin. If you were a gentleman, you'd give the space to Veronica," Ruby said.

"Please, I'm fine here. Don't trouble yourself," I said to Todd as he shuffled in the bed and blushed.

Todd continued to look a little shamefaced. "I didn't think. Maybe I was whacked on the head harder than I realised."

"Maybe it knocked some sense into you," Ruby said. "Leaving your door unlocked! Whatever next?"

Todd pulled a face. "This is a safe neighbourhood. Nothing bad ever happens around here, unless you count a few pints of milk being scooped off porch steps and Old Father Joe's bicycle being stolen by children, but that was months ago."

"A little less bickering may help my headache," I whispered.

"See! Now you've upset Veronica." Ruby thumped Todd while I closed my eyes and resigned myself to the headache.

Thirty minutes later, and after two strong restorative cups of tea and a small brandy, I felt better. The headache was subsiding, and Ruby had cleaned the blood off my forehead and the dirt off my face and out of my hair, so I felt partway normal.

There was a knock on the door.

"That must be the police." Peter hurried off to let them in.

Inspector Templeton strode into the bedroom a moment later with his colleague, Sergeant Matthers.

"Is it just the two of you?" I peered past them. "A potential killer is on the loose around here."

"There is a team doing door-to-door enquiries." Inspector Templeton's gaze was fixed on my head wound. "Right, you're straight off to the hospital."

I held up my hands. "Not just yet. Ruby and Peter have been taking the best care of us. It's important we find out who did this."

"Veronica! You're clearly injured." He hovered a hand close to me, but it didn't make contact.

"I have a small cut and a bump on my head. I'm very capable of talking."

Inspector Templeton grumbled his disapproval, failing to mask the worry in his eyes.

"I will go to the hospital once I've furnished you with all the information. Speed of action is most important in this situation. Our attacker has over thirty minutes on you," I said.

With a resigned sigh, Inspector Templeton took out his notepad. "Give me the details so my officers can keep a lookout."

We recounted our less-than-helpful description of our assailant and talked through the attack. I sensed growing frustration, but there was nothing I could do to be more useful. If I'd anticipated the assault with a tree branch, I'd have been more alert, but I'd come to Todd's for a friendly evening of low-key sleuthing, not with the intention of adding a new scar to my collection.

Inspector Templeton tucked away his notepad. "I've got everything I can. Now, you need to go to the hospital. The ambulance has arrived and will take you both."

"I've suffered more serious injuries than this and didn't visit the hospital," I said.

"I must admit, I am feeling queasy," Todd said. "It could be the shock, but perhaps being checked over by an attractive nurse would set me to rights."

"Don't joke about something so serious. Head injuries aren't to be taken lightly." Ruby turned to me. "Please, go in the ambulance. It's better to be safe than sorry. Besides, you know how much I adore a handsome doctor."

Although I could be stubborn, I wasn't foolish, and head wounds needed to be treated with the proper level of respect. "I'll go, to ensure you don't worry unnecessarily. And, of course, to find you a nice doctor friend."

Ruby grinned. "That's the spirit."

Sergeant Matthers assisted Todd while Ruby looked after me.

I turned as we were leaving the room. Benji sat by the side of the bed. "Come on, boy."

"He can't go in the ambulance," Inspector Templeton said.

"I'm not leaving him behind."

He studied Benji for a second. "Benji can ride with me."

"That's considerate of you. Thank you." I felt almost tearful at his show of kindness. It must be a side effect of my head injury.

Benji stood, stamped his paws on the floor, and barked.

Inspector Templeton frowned. "But he can only ride with me if he's well-behaved."

"Benji is always well-behaved."

"He's crawling under the bed!"

"He's free-spirited and excited that we're going on an adventure," I said. "Benji, this way. It's time to leave."

It took a moment of cajoling before Benji finally wriggled out from underneath Todd's bed and followed us outside. His wagging tail stopped when he realised we were to be separated. I promised him we wouldn't be parted for long, encouraged him into Inspector Templeton's car, and then closed the door.

As the car drove away, I saw not only Benji's worried face but also Inspector Templeton's. The man was worrying about nothing. So was the adorable dog.

My head throbbed, and I closed my eyes and touched my forehead.

"Let's get you looked at by a professional, and then it's time to rest," Ruby said quietly. "We've all had quite enough excitement for one day."

"Yes," I murmured. "I believe you're right. Let's find you a handsome doctor, and me some strong pain relief."

Chapter 16

"Follow the light with your eyes." A charming doctor named George Knight had been examining me for ten minutes. He'd checked my temperature, pulse, reflexes, and was repeating checks on my vision to ensure he'd missed nothing untoward.

Much to Ruby's delight, he was tall, dark, and handsome, and looked splendid in his white doctor's coat, but I was still mulling over recent events, so barely noticed his charm.

"Veronica will live, won't she, doctor?" Ruby asked.

"I'm happy to say, other than a sore head, Miss Vale appears to have the constitution of an ox." Doctor Knight pocketed his small torch and smiled at me. "There's no need for you to stay overnight in the hospital."

"I informed my friends and the police of my ox-like constitution, but no one listened to me," I said. "I'm sorry to have wasted your time."

Doctor Knight's smile broadened. "Perhaps you should have trained in the profession, since you appear to be an expert in all things medical."

"I'll stick to what I do best, but thank you for giving me a clean bill of health." I eased myself off the examination couch.

Doctor Knight assisted me with a hand on my elbow. "I want you to take it easy and rest for the evening. Do you live alone?"

"Doctor! Is that a proposition?" Ruby asked.

He chuckled. "Patients with head injuries can't be left alone overnight and need to be checked on."

"I live with my mother and my younger brother," I said.

"You don't want to bother them, though," Ruby said. "I'm happy to stay with you. We can bunk in the same bed since you have such an enormous double all to yourself."

"Hardly. I share it with Benji."

"Benji is your fiancé?" Doctor Knight asked.

"Her dog," Ruby said. "Veronica is single and available. Put a note of that on her record and be sure to tell all of your suitable friends. I'm available, too."

"Stop bothering the good doctor, or he'll have you admitted to a psychiatric unit," I said.

"That's quite all right, Miss Vale." Doctor Knight did indeed write something on my notes, but I doubted it had anything to do with our availability. "If Miss Smythe could stay with you overnight, it would be a weight off my mind."

"I'll check Veronica every hour," Ruby said. "Do I need to wake her?"

"No, but ensure she's comfortable and her breathing is steady. But there's really no need for concern."

"Does that mean I'm free to go?" I asked.

"Give me a few minutes to finish the paperwork, and you can be on your way." Doctor Knight nodded at us and left the room.

"I'm glad that's over," I said. "Make yourself useful and find Peter."

"What do you want with him?" Ruby asked.

"While we have nothing to do, we can pick up where we left off. If things had gone according to plan, I would have been interrogating Peter over a gin fizz about the night of Arthur's murder."

"The last time I saw him, he was in the corridor, outside Todd's room. He was flirting with a nurse! I'll be right back." Ruby dashed out of the room.

I let out a soft sigh. I was glad I had no health concerns, but I would have an impressive bruise, and it would send my mother into palpitations for weeks every time she looked at the cut on my forehead. Perhaps I'd fashion my hair so she wouldn't notice. I'd pick up a magazine the next time I was out and get some inspiration. There must be a style that hid a head wound.

Ruby reappeared, towing Peter behind her.

"How is the patient?" he asked, ducking to examine my head. "You look much better than when we first found you."

"I'm recovering well, thank you. How is Todd?"

"The doctor is happy with him," Peter said. "Gosh! This is all a bit of a shocker. I didn't expect to end up at the hospital this evening."

"Neither did I. Although I will confess, you received an invitation to Todd's because I had an ulterior motive to see you again." I was too tired to beat around the bush.

"What was your motive?" Peter appeared intrigued.

"I wanted to ask about your argument with Arthur at the party," I said.

Peter tucked his hands into his trouser pockets. "What about it? There's not much to tell."

"Which means it won't take you long to share."

He shrugged. "I thought Arthur had sunk one of my billiard balls. And I thought he took a turn when he shouldn't have. I wasn't paying attention. I had my eye on a young lady at the party, but she got talking to someone else and I was jealous. I took my bad mood out on Arthur. We both made idiots of ourselves. Blame the champagne. Voices got raised."

"What did you do?"

"He chased me around the table several times until I jumped out the window. I landed in a bush and trampled the poor thing to death. When I came to my senses, I realised what a buffoon I'd made of myself, so I walked around the garden to figure out a plan to win the hand of the lady I hoped to charm."

"I can't imagine seeing you arguing with Arthur and then jumping out of the window in terror will have put her off," Ruby said tartly.

"After you gave me the brush-off, I had no choice but to try my luck elsewhere." Peter laughed with a mixture of self-effacing embarrassment. "I must have been outside for longer than I thought I was, because when I returned, she'd gone off with someone else. I missed my chance."

"Bad luck," I said. "We were sad to learn what happened to Arthur. Do you have any thoughts about it?"

Peter was quiet for a long time, staring at a cabinet of medical equipment. "I still don't believe it. I've known him since we were children. It makes no sense."

"I didn't realise you were close." Ruby touched his arm. "We really are sorry for your loss."

"I appreciate that. Damned shame." Peter blinked rapidly. "I know what people have been saying about your brother, but I don't believe Todd had anything to do with it."

"That's good of you to say," Ruby said. "I had to assume you consider him innocent since you were happy to visit his home."

Peter tipped his head from side to side. "I had an ulterior motive, too. I like Todd, but I wanted to ask questions about his fight with Arthur, and figure out why things got bad between them. They're usually the life and soul of any party. I... I don't like to gossip, but I'm aware Todd has money troubles, and he was angry because Arthur wouldn't help him."

"You saw their fight?" I asked.

Peter nodded. "Todd desperately needed easy cash fast, but Arthur blocked access to Lady Sybil's money. I heard him say she'd never give Todd a bean, and the family wasn't financially sensible."

Ruby emitted an unladylike noise of dissent. "You make it sound like we're destitute."

"Sorry, I meant no offence," Peter said. "Most of what I've heard is rumour, so I don't know what's true."

"Could you elaborate on those rumours?" I asked.

Peter pursed his lips and considered his answer. "I've heard Todd was jealous of Arthur. He had it all. An attractive, older woman who was introducing him to the right people and supporting his lifestyle. He had the freedom to take risks at work because he didn't need to worry about getting things wrong, since he had Lady Sybil's protection."

"She is a formidable lady," I said.

"And more influential than a lot of us realise," Peter said. "Her late husband's name wields power. He was something important during the war and earned a lot of respect. Arthur was happy to take advantage of Lady Sybil's influence."

"Only with her approval," I said. "She doesn't strike me as a lady to be easily influenced, no matter how handsome the face."

"I'm certain of it," Peter said. "She willingly financed Arthur's excesses, though. He was showing off the latest watch she gifted him. That's one new watch a month since they became involved."

"Todd wouldn't be jealous over such frippery," Ruby said.

"Perhaps not, but Arthur sometimes rubbed our noses in it. He could be hard on Todd, and from what I know of Todd's situation, if not destitute, he is down on his luck."

"Just because my brother has had a bad run of things, it doesn't turn him into a killer," Ruby said. "Todd and Arthur have always been friends."

"I know! Which is why I was so surprised when the police took him in for questioning," Peter said. "Then I recalled Todd's comment a few weeks ago about if only he could have a Lady Sybil of his own, then his life would be dandy. It got me wondering."

"Did you share your wonderings with the police?" I asked. "Was that why they were so swift to take Todd in and consider him the main suspect in Arthur's murder?"

"Goodness! No. I'd never tittle-tattle on a friend. I was looking at it from an outsider's point of view. If a person didn't know Todd and Arthur, it would be the conclusion they'd come to with the information we have. There was a serious fight, and that same evening, Arthur died."

Ruby grabbed her handbag. "If you'll excuse me, I need to use the lavatory." She dashed out, and the door shut behind her.

"I'm sorry. I didn't want to upset Ruby." Peter rubbed the back of his neck. "Everyone is flummoxed as to what happened to Arthur. I wasn't thinking, but I thought it might help to talk through my concerns."

"I'm flummoxed too. Todd is adamant he is innocent, though."

"I don't doubt he is," Peter said. "But who does that leave the police?"

"Perhaps you saw something at the party," I said. "Something the police have overlooked."

He shrugged. "I don't recall seeing anything out of the ordinary. I spent the early part of the party with Todd, Arthur, Ruby, and a few other acquaintances, but after Ruby cooled on me, my attention went to the other young lady. She was a cracker. After I lost sight of her, I played a few more rounds of billiards and stayed up late drinking."

"You were in the games room all night?"

"Not at first. I danced and mingled, but as the party progressed, I moved in there. It was stifling hot in some of the rooms with all the bodies crammed together,"

Peter said. "I played a few rounds with Arthur, Todd, and a couple of other chaps. Got so blotto, I accidentally tore the cloth during a bungled shot. If there was any funny business going on, I didn't see it."

"Apart from the fight between Todd and Arthur?" I narrowed my eyes. Was it mere coincidence that the only unusual event Peter witnessed ensured Todd remained the prime suspect in this investigation? Perhaps Peter had something to hide, but he realised with the odds stacked against Todd, by adding fuel to the fire, no one would look his way.

"I should have paid more attention," Peter said. "I'd have seen someone behaving strangely around Arthur and stopped things going so far."

"Perhaps, but the police have yet to discover the motive for Arthur's murder."

"It's a baffling case, that's for sure," Peter said. "I'd hate to be in Todd's shoes. He's had a string of rotten luck. He can't hold down a decent job. He has no joy with the ladies, and then to be attacked in his own home. What is the world coming to?"

"That is an excellent question," I said. "Why would someone make so much effort to silence Todd?"

Peter looked at me. "What do you think is going on?"

"I wish I knew." I gently rubbed my forehead as my headache returned. "I really wish I knew."

Chapter 17

"Are you sure you shouldn't stay in bed?" True to her word, Ruby had spent the night being an absolute pest. She'd insisted we sleep in the same bed, my large double, and had alternated between prodding me in the arm and blowing on my face at hourly intervals to ensure I hadn't expired during the night.

"I'm tempted to stay here since you make such a terrible bedfellow." I slid my foot into a sensible shoe. "But we have a murder to solve."

Ruby borrowed my face cream and applied it liberally to not only her face but also her arms, rubbing generous amounts on her elbows. "Todd is free! He may be in the hospital, feeling sorry for himself, but you made the police let him go."

"That's a temporary reprieve," I said. "Inspector Templeton still has Todd as the prime suspect."

"Surely not. After what happened yesterday, it proves there's a maniac on the loose targeting Arthur and his friends. We've been looking at this all wrong."

"What reason does this mysterious maniac have for picking on this friendship group?" I stroked Benji's head.

Pippin lay beside him, content to sleep while we talked. She was such a sweet little dog.

"We need to question Todd and Peter and anyone else associated with them to find the connection," Ruby said. "Maybe it's something to do with their education? Or their work?"

"That sounds like an awful lot of trouble. And I'm unsure it'll take us in the right direction."

"What else could it be?" Ruby examined the small amount of makeup I had on my dressing table. "Don't you have any Rimmel cake?"

"I go for the basics, so no mascara. I make do with my postman face. I don't want to scare the poor chap when he delivers the letters, but I also don't want to be mistaken for a dancing girl with too much colour and flare when I open the door to collect a parcel."

"I love the bright colours! I'll have to get you something special for your birthday." Ruby rifled through my drawers in the hope of finding a hidden stash of makeup. She would be disappointed.

"Save your pennies," I said. "And focus on the finger of suspicion pointing firmly at Todd."

"Perhaps Inspector Templeton will give us an update this morning." Ruby thoroughly covered her face with powder. "The house-to-house enquiries must have turned up something useful."

"As we've come to realise, Inspector Templeton doesn't rush to inform us about what's going on in any investigation we assist with."

Ruby grinned at me. "I can't imagine why. We're the most useful volunteer officers he has! I'd suggest he give us uniforms, but even with my curves, I wouldn't be able to pull off such dismal attire. And think of the mess such a cumbersome hat would make of my hair."

"Are you girls awake?" Mother tapped on my door, surprising me because she was out of bed so early. She pushed open the door and gasped. "Veronica! You should be tucked under your covers and resting with a warm compress on your forehead. Don't think for one second, you're leaving this house after everything you've been through."

When we'd returned home the previous evening, as I'd predicted, my mother had forty fits due to my mild injury. She demanded a full debrief, and just about passed out in shock by the time I'd finished. Despite my assurances I was well and a small bump on the head wouldn't slow me, she'd insisted I go to bed and not get out of it for at least two weeks.

"I took the best care of Veronica," Ruby said, "and made sure she got through the night."

"I didn't sleep for worrying you'd weaken and not see daybreak." My mother inched into the room, wielding a walking stick. "I told Matthew to sit by your door all night in case you needed anything. Where is that boy?"

"As soon as I realised what you'd done, I sent him to bed," I said. "Matthew doesn't need to suffer because I didn't pay attention."

"He is your brother. He's supposed to look after you." My mother poked her head back out the door and hollered his name.

"Leave him alone," I said. "He needs sleep, too. I have Ruby with me, and Benji and Pippin. They make the best nurses. Although my arm is sore from where Ruby kept poking me to make sure I was still breathing. A small compact mirror held under my nose would have achieved the same thing, without any bruising."

"I had to be doubly sure you weren't dead! You can never be too careful with head wounds." Ruby gave up searching for more makeup and tested my scant amount of fragrance.

"Which is exactly my point," my mother said. "Back into bed. I'll get Matthew up to fix a nice breakfast for all of us, and I'll sit and check your pulse for irregularities."

I inspected my reflection in the mirror as I tidied my hair, doing an ineffective job of concealing the large bruise that had bloomed. "I'll feel better when I'm doing something. If I stay in bed, I'll keep worrying about the murder investigation and whether the police will be waiting for Todd when he gets out of the hospital."

"It's far too dangerous for you to remain involved," my mother said. "Ruby, help me talk some sense into her."

"If I could achieve such a feat, I'd have done it a long time ago," Ruby said. "When Veronica wants to do something, she'll do it."

My mother sighed and tutted. "And leaves my nerves in pieces on the floor to be eaten by some feral kitten."

I held in a sigh. Mother only complained because she cared, but it vexed my already strained nerves after a poor night of sleep. "I'll take it easy. But I have an early appointment to get to."

"Where are we going?" Ruby asked.

"You're going to see Todd at the hospital," I said. "I telephoned Lady Sybil's residence first thing and made an appointment with the lady of the house."

"When did you do that?"

"While you slept."

"I didn't close my eyes all night."

"You roused me with your snoring on two occasions."

Ruby sniffed a bottle of fragrance. "You sound delusional. That bump on the head must be more serious than we realised."

"Don't say that." I shot a look at my quivering mother.

"I should come with you." Ruby finished spritzing herself with my perfume and set down the bottle.

"You must want to see how Todd is getting on," I said. "If he had a comfortable night, they'll release him today, but he'll need someone to keep an eye on him."

Ruby groaned. "He's so annoying. Why couldn't he have taken down his attacker rather than leaving it to you and Benji?"

My mother waved a hand in front of her face. "All this talk of attackers makes me feel faint. Where is Matthew with our restorative pot of tea?"

"Lay on the bed and Benji will lick your face. That'll restore you." Although I felt better, the tree branch had knocked all patience out of my head, so my words were sharper than I'd intended.

"I'm surprised Lady Sybil is prepared to see you again," Ruby said. "After your last visit, you didn't leave on the best of terms."

"I may have embellished my reason for wanting to visit again," I said. "The last time we met, she was interested in placing an advertisement for a new partner to replace Arthur."

"When her previous partner has yet to be buried!" my mother exclaimed. "The cheek of the woman."

"Lady Sybil is practical. And it's not uncommon for single people to place advertisements when looking for a companion," I said. "It's become popular since the war ended. Many ladies find it hard to find suitable bachelors with so many men lost on the battlefield."

"Such a dreadful thing," my mother said. "We should go back to the days of formal balls and introductions. Parents were involved in making the matches, so there was no need for this nonsense."

"Times have changed, and I'm glad of that," I said. "While we're discussing advertisements, I intend to question Lady Sybil about how fiery the relationship was, and see if she lets anything slip."

"I don't like this one bit." Mother looked up. "Matthew! There you are. We're all expiring from hunger."

"There's no time for breakfast," I said, before Matthew had a chance to blink the sleep from his eyes.

Ruby pouted. "I'm famished."

"Perhaps your charming doctor could muster you a cup of tea and a piece of toast when you visit Todd. Let's hurry. There are too many unanswered questions in this mystery, and we need to change that."

I kissed my mother's cheek as she continued to protest about me leaving, but she was distracted by Matthew, who was bumbling around, holding two kittens while stroking Pippin and asking if she wanted toast with her cereal or if porridge was worth the effort.

"Veronica! Aren't you taking Benji?" my mother called out.

"He can keep you company today with Pippin. I'll be back to collect him later."

"I meant to tell you, when Inspector Templeton dropped him off, he was eating something."

"Benji or Inspector Templeton?"

"Benji! He wouldn't let me see what it was."

"It was most likely a treat," I said, my hand on the door. "Inspector Templeton can be grumpy, but he is dreadfully fond of Benji, and he has a bag of dog chews in his car, which he sneaks to Benji when he thinks I'm not looking."

"Whatever the treat was, Benji kept chewing it."

"Benji has the constitution of a wolf, so it won't do him harm to have a challenging treat to occupy his time. I'll catch up with you later." I hurried Ruby out of the front door before my mother could make any more excuses to keep me at home. I was hailing a taxi when a plain black car pulled up beside us. Inspector Templeton was inside.

"This is a surprise," I murmured.

"Do you think it's bad news if he's come to give us an update in person?" Ruby's bright expression faded.

"He doesn't look happy, but he usually frowns when he's around me." I tapped on the car window. "Good day, Inspector. What do we owe this early morning delight?"

He wound down the window. "Shouldn't you be in bed?"

"You sound like my mother. I'm as fit as a fiddle, and a small cut on the head won't stop me."

"I imagine handcuffs and solitary confinement wouldn't stop you either when you set your mind to something," Inspector Templeton said.

"How well you know me. What news from yesterday?"

"That's what I'm here to talk to you about. I made a detour on my way to work."

"Did you find the man who attacked Todd and Veronica?" Ruby peered through the open window.

Inspector Templeton shook his head. "We searched the gardens and knocked on doors of local neighbours. Nobody saw a thing."

"How disappointing," I said. "No clues inside Todd's lodgings?"

"If there had been, I've no doubt you would have discovered them before us," Inspector Templeton said.

"I'd normally agree, but I wasn't on my best form." I glanced up as a taxi zoomed past. "If you'll excuse us, Inspector, we have things to do."

"I'm aware. It's the other reason I'm here. I received a disgruntled telephone call at home from Lady Sybil. She said you demanded to question her and asked me if these questions were in any way official."

Oh dear. Caught out again. "I have business with Lady Sybil. And I was considering asking her innocent questions about Arthur while conducting said business. In case you've forgotten, I'm writing Arthur's obituary, so I need pertinent information."

"Lady Sybil was under the impression you'd be questioning her as a suspect in Arthur's murder. Why would that be?"

"A guilty conscience!" Ruby exclaimed. "The woman hasn't been truthful about her relationship with Arthur."

"Which is why I'm accompanying you to Lady Sybil's," Inspector Templeton said.

"There's no need," I replied.

"Since you've put yourself in the role of lead investigator in this murder, I have no option but to shadow you," Inspector Templeton said. "If you collect a statement or evidence, I must be there."

"Does that mean you're not arresting Todd once he's discharged from the hospital?" Ruby's tone was tinged with hopeful joy.

"As of this moment, not yet. But he's still not in the clear."

"After everything we've done to help you, he should be." Ruby turned to me. "I'd come with you, but you're right about me visiting the hospital. Even if it's just to ensure Todd's not bothering too many nurses. And I want to see if I can get that charming doctor's telephone number."

"Since I'm now in Inspector Templeton's mainly capable hands, you go to the hospital, and I'll visit Lady Sybil. That's assuming you'll let me into your vehicle, Inspector."

He glowered at me. "Get in. We don't want to be late."

I bid goodbye to Ruby and climbed into Inspector Templeton's car, which was designed for efficiency rather than luxury or comfort, the faint smell of oil in the air.

Inspector Templeton pulled out into the growing traffic, the buses full of people heading into work.

"Have you any thoughts about what happened at Todd's yesterday?" I asked when the silence grew too intense to be comfortable.

"We're working on some theories."

"Is one of those theories that Todd is innocent, and the person who attacked him could also have murdered Arthur?"

"That's one theory. We're also wondering if Todd set up the attack to shift suspicion from him."

I turned in my seat. "That's scandalous!"

"His injury wasn't as severe as yours," Inspector Templeton said. "It suggests his attacker wasn't serious about completing the job. And the methods of murder are different. Todd was attacked and hit on the back of the head. Whereas Arthur..." he pressed his lips together.

"Please, continue. You have yet to disclose how Arthur died, no matter how many times I ask. If the rumour is true, it was suffocation."

Inspector Templeton grumbled under his breath. "You know too much."

I slapped a hand against my thigh. "It makes perfect sense. No weapon in the room, no blood on the body, and the only injuries were a few bruises. Arthur would have been drunk, so I doubt he struggled much. Although the ripped pillow suggests he tried his best."

Inspector Templeton tapped his finger on the steering wheel. "It was suffocation. Which proves it's unlikely to be the same person who attacked Todd and Arthur."

"Or the person who murdered Arthur planned the same method on Todd, but I disturbed him," I said.

"It's something to consider." Inspector Templeton manoeuvred through the traffic, taking us away from the bustle of the London streets and through the quiet suburbs as we headed to Lady Sybil's. "Talk to me about your other suspects."

"Is this in my role as an expert consultant?"

"Do not try my patience," he said through gritted teeth. "I could have you locked up for poking about in this investigation."

"I am most willing to share." I didn't bother to hide my smile, since Inspector Templeton's attention was on the road. "We'll start with Todd. I know his character well. He's innocent. He makes foolish decisions, but he's one of the most kind-hearted people I know."

"Kind-hearted enough to have a serious fight with Arthur?"

"He can be a touch immature, but Todd's not malicious. He's always bickering with Ruby, but the next day, they're the best of friends. Todd doesn't hold a grudge about anything."

"He has no alibi."

"There were several pleasant men in the park where he slept who verify he was there."

"They're unreliable witnesses. And we can't trace the taxi who took him home. Could that be because he's lying?"

Inspector Templeton wasn't budging from his obsession with Todd. "We also have Peter Appleby. His alibi needs checking."

"I've spoken to members of the household. It wasn't Peter. He was asleep."

"Lady Sybil's Uncle John pointed the finger at Peter. And when I questioned him at the hospital yesterday—"

"You were questioning Peter while being treated for a head injury?"

"I have the ability to do more than one task at a time," I said. "Peter seemed genuinely remorseful. I wonder about him, though. He was keen to put Todd back in the frame by debating about the severity of the fight he had with Arthur."

"Despite your protestations, Todd is still my prime suspect."

"Then I'll have to protest louder."

We drove for several minutes in another tense silence.

"What about Lady Sybil?" I asked. "She concealed the intensity of her argument with Arthur. Why do that if she had nothing to hide?"

"To avoid an embarrassment? And Lady Sybil has an alibi. Her lady's maid saw her to bed."

"But did Lady Sybil remain in bed once Alice put her there?"

Inspector Templeton remained silent.

"Arthur's sister, Emma Wainwright, was also at the party. I met her in the gardens and thought highly of her, but she didn't approve of her brother's reckless ways, nor his involvement with Lady Sybil."

"Emma retired for the night after assisting John to bed," Inspector Templeton said. "Despite you thinking I don't know how to do my job, I'm a competent questioner."

"I never said you couldn't do your job," I said. "But I look at things from a different angle and give you an alternative perspective."

"Your alternative perspective is biased because you refuse to believe Todd Smythe could be a killer."

I wasn't prepared to dignify that foolishness with an answer.

"We also have our mysterious attacker," I said. "A plump, average-height man. Ruby suggested it could be someone attacking Arthur and his friends, but why?"

"That would lead us into a whole other investigation. It would be foolhardy to pursue the theory."

"My thoughts exactly," I said.

Inspector Templeton was silent for a full minute. "We agree on something?"

"Stranger things have happened."

"Not to me."

I tutted and admired the Rolls Royce we drove past.

"Veronica, leave this investigation to the experts," Inspector Templeton said.

"I'm here now. We're barely fifteen minutes from Lady Sybil's. And you know I can be useful."

He slid me a glance. "I'm never getting rid of you, am I?"

I smiled sweetly at him. "Only when I choose to go. These days, a lady has a right to choose many things."

We turned onto a pleasant country lane, and I spent a moment enjoying the view of green fields and flashes of springtime buds.

"How's the head feeling now you're out and about?" Inspector Templeton asked. "It's not too late to return home."

"It is. And my head is perfectly fine."

"Despite being knocked senseless yesterday, you look remarkably well."

I turned and stared at him. "Was that a compliment?"

"I'm allowed to give an attractive single woman a compliment, aren't I?"

My cheeks heated, and I busied myself with my handbag.

Inspector Templeton chuckled. "Veronica Vale, lost for words. I should say nice things to you more often."

"Do be quiet, Inspector." I snapped my handbag shut. "And let's go catch our killer."

Chapter 18

Lady Sybil's butler announced us, and I walked into the sitting room with Inspector Templeton beside me.

She wore a dropped waist gray silk dress with fine lace embroidery around the neckline, and was seated by the window where we'd had our last conversation. When she saw who I was with, a flicker of amusement crossed her face. The plucky lady had ensured we wouldn't be meeting alone.

"Did you encounter each other on your way in?" she asked, as she civilly greeted us.

"We travelled here together," I said. "I have experience of working with the police, and they often put my services to good use."

Inspector Templeton made a noise of disagreement.

"I suppose your work as an obituary writer must weave your paths together." Lady Sybil gestured for us to take seats. "Have you had breakfast?"

"It was an early start for me this morning," Inspector Templeton said. "But please, don't trouble yourself."

"I could eat something," I said.

Lady Sybil's gaze shifted to concern as she noticed my head injury. "What have you been getting yourself into?"

"It looks worse than it is," I said. "I was hit on the head with a tree branch when stopping Todd Smythe from being killed."

"Veronica!" Inspector Templeton said. "Let's not trouble Lady Sybil with unnecessary details."

Lady Sybil had risen and pulled the cord by the door before returning to her seat. "I'm intrigued. And I want to be troubled."

I briefly relayed the events that led to my impressive bruise under Inspector Templeton's steely glare. I concluded by saying I believed Arthur's murder and Todd's attack could be connected.

"The same man who killed Arthur attempted to take Todd's life? Why?" Lady Sybil showed round-eyed surprise.

"We don't know that for certain," Inspector Templeton said sharply. "Veronica is working on a theory, but we have plenty of others."

Lady Sybil pressed a hand against her chest and took in a deep breath. "I'm stunned. I must admit, Arthur's death disappointed me, but to know his attacker had some vexatious plan to harm others. It's unthinkable."

"Yes, it is unthinkable, and also unlikely," Inspector Templeton said. "It's more likely the two attacks are unrelated."

"I'm keeping an open mind until justice is served," I said.

Lady Sybil paused our conversation as Alice appeared with another servant, and we were provided with tea, warm crumpets, pots of raspberry jam, butter, and bowls of fresh fruit.

We exchanged pleasantries while we ate, commenting on the weather and the view from the sitting room, but my mind was occupied with more taxing thoughts. Lady Sybil had seemed shocked by the thought of a killer on the loose. Was she so surprised because she knew who had killed Arthur and she hadn't expected an attack on Todd? Or was there no connection between the two?

"How is Todd following his beating?" Lady Sybil asked.

"He should get out of the hospital today," I said. "His sister is looking after him."

"It was serious enough for him to need medical assistance?"

"It was. And although Inspector Templeton has other theories, I believe there was malice behind the attack. If my dog hadn't alerted me to the fight, Todd may not have survived."

"Does Todd have a sweetheart?" Lady Sybil asked. "Perhaps it was an attack from a former beau. Todd could have ruffled feathers. He's almost as handsome as Arthur was, and I saw the ladies casting admiring glances his way at the party."

"Todd hasn't had a serious relationship for some time," I said. "He's not always sensible about his choice of companion."

"How unfortunate for him. I must admit, I've never seen him with a particular lady at any of my gatherings," Lady Sybil said. "He's friendly to everyone. It's a shame he's not settled."

"When the right woman appears, I'm sure he will," I said. "Just as I'm sure you'll find a suitable replacement for Arthur."

A faint smirk flashed across Lady Sybil's face. "Ah, yes. Your ruse about wanting to visit to discuss the advertisement in your newspaper."

"It wasn't a ruse. I'm happy to talk about the price and wording so you can find a new gentleman friend," I said. "There is space in the newspaper to include your advertisement."

Lady Sybil sipped her tea. "When your message was relayed to me about the purpose of your visit, I had to smile. I am aware of your connection to the Smythe family, so I knew you had ulterior motives."

"Which is why you contacted Inspector Templeton," I said. "You were concerned I would misbehave?"

"I don't enjoy being put on the back foot," Lady Sybil said. "And since I have nothing to hide, I was happy for the police to be in attendance. Make sure everything is done by the book."

"Since we are all such open books, would you be happy to answer questions about your relationship with Arthur?" I asked. "Specifically, why you downplayed how serious your argument was on the night of his death?""Veronica, allow me to lead on the questioning in regards to the investigation," Inspector Templeton said.

I gestured for him to speak with a terse hand movement. He would ask the same thing, so I was saving us both time.

Lady Sybil set down her cup. "I wasn't proud of my behaviour. I had grown concerned Arthur was tiring of me. We'd been bickering frequently, and I believe he intended to leave me."

"You didn't want that to happen?" I asked.

Inspector Templeton sighed as I took the lead again, but didn't attempt to stop me.

"Arthur was adorable. And he made me look good when he was on my arm."

"How serious was the relationship?" Inspector Templeton asked. "Was there talk of marriage?"

"I have been married once, and that was enough to last me a lifetime," Lady Sybil said.

"When I spoke to you about your relationship with Arthur, you said he adored you and had no interest in the material offerings you provided. Was that the truth?" I asked.

Lady Sybil's gaze turned to the window. "I always hoped Arthur would mature. Of course, my wealth and status initially dazzled him, so I'm sure those things made me much more attractive. But I have a pleasant character. I'm entertaining, intelligent, and an excellent dinner conversationalist. I wanted him to be pleased by those aspects, too."

"He wasn't?" I asked.

"Arthur wasn't mature enough to recognise my qualities," Lady Sybil said. "It was a pity because he had prospects. Still, he was an exceedingly handsome man, and I was the envy of all of my friends. If he was with me because of my money rather than my character, I was willing to accept that."

"You really didn't mind?"

Lady Sybil turned back to me with a resolved expression on her face. "Miss Vale, I deserve happiness. The war took so much from all of us, and I despise that. I despise war. It's such a cruel event. So much loss and tragedy."

"It was a terrible time for all of us," I said.

Lady Sybil stood and collected photographs from a side cabinet, which she brought over and showed to us. "My two sons. My boys were my proudest achievement. They were strong, handsome, capable men. The war took from me them. I recognise we needed to protect ourselves, but the Great War was a terrible thing."

I studied the photographs of her sons. "It's rare to find someone who didn't experience tragedy during that time."

Lady Sybil took the framed pictures and returned them to their original place, and then sat in her seat. "Did you serve in some capacity?"

I nodded. "I did my bit. There was a stint on the exchange network, but my duties were matched to fit my capabilities."

Curiosity lit Lady Sybil's eyes. "I would be most interested in hearing about that at a more appropriate time."

"I don't like to dwell on the past," I said.

"Of course. Some things need to be kept under wraps." Lady Sybil's gaze flicked from me. "Inspector?"

"I was there. It was a difficult time. I'm sorry so many people you cared about were taken from you."

"As am I. I'm glad it's all over," Lady Sybil said. "People can have fun again without the threat of war looming over their heads. And Arthur was so much fun, even though he couldn't handle his drink, and he had a bit of a temper."

"Did Arthur's temper ever scare you?" I asked.

She scoffed out a laugh. "Never! These young men are all the same, more bluff and warm wind than anything concerning. Perhaps I should find myself a more mature type." Her gaze settled on Inspector Templeton. "Are you single, Inspector?"

I was able to stop from laughing by stuffing a crumpet into my mouth, although it sounded like I was choking for a few seconds.

"Come now, there's no need to be shy." A smile played on Lady Sybil's lips. "There's only a few years' difference in age, and there would be far less gossip if I had you on my arm rather than some bright young thing."

Inspector Templeton's cheeks were deep crimson as he made notes on his pad. "Your attention is flattering, Lady Sybil, but I am dedicated to my work."

"No Mrs Templeton? Interesting." Lady Sybil's gaze slid to me. "You have jam on the corner of your mouth, my dear."

I dabbed it away and swallowed the last of my crumpet.

Alice entered the room. "There's a telephone call for you, Lady Sybil."

"If you'll excuse me a moment." Lady Sybil left the room, and Alice cleared our breakfast things.

"Alice, would it be possible to visit the games' room?" I asked.

"Of course, miss," Alice said. "I can take you there if you'd like to follow me."

"Why do you want to see that room?" Inspector Templeton asked as we followed Alice along a smartly decorated hallway.

"Peter said he was up late playing billiards and drinking. He admits to damaging the cloth on the table because he was so drunk. If we can confirm that, it may eliminate him from our enquiries. If he was so drunk, he was unable to hit a cue ball, the chances are, he wouldn't have been able to creep along country lanes, sneak into the Drunken Duck, and suffocate Arthur."

Inspector Templeton grumbled to himself. He may have muttered about me being stubborn and not listening to him. The delicious crumpets and tea had clearly not improved his mood.

We arrived in the games' room, and Alice showed us the billiards table. Sure enough, there was a large tear in the felt, which she explained had been done during the party, although she hadn't seen who'd done it.

"Did a guest called Peter Appleby stay at the house that night?" I asked.

"He did. I don't always remember the guests' names," Alice said, "but I did a final check on the hallways before turning in for the night. I stood outside Mr Appleby's door listening to the most extraordinary noise."

"What noise would that be?" I asked.

"Snoring! At first, I thought there was an unhappy pig in his room, but I peeked inside, and he was flat on his back, fully clothed, his arms and legs splayed, making such a racket. I thought he'd wake the rest of the household." Alice giggled, then blushed.

"I could have told you that," Inspector Templeton murmured.

"There's no harm in double-checking facts. Thank you, Alice. That's most useful," I said. "One more thing. I have a question about your friendship with Arthur. You were firm in stating you had no fond relations with him. Was that the truth?"

"Blimey, you a copper, too, miss?" Alice asked, all wide-eyed and mouth agape.

"No, nor shall she ever be," Inspector Templeton said.

"I am as good as you, if not better, despite receiving no formal training," I said tartly. "Alice, I would appreciate an answer."

She blushed again, but shook her head. "I was fond of Arthur, and he flirted something terrible, but there was nothing between us. I value my job too much to risk getting involved with him. Besides, you get to know that type. Arthur would flirt with the chimney sweep and the milk maid and never meant nothing by it. And I've started walking out with the butcher's apprentice from down the road. He's ever so handsome. He bought me a posy of flowers this morning."

"I appreciate your honesty," I said. "That'll be all."

The second Alice was gone, Inspector Templeton rounded on me. "You cannot keep pushing your way into this investigation. I brought you here as a courtesy because I was concerned about your head injury and didn't want you overexerting yourself. But you are acting beyond your boundaries."

I peered at the torn billiard cloth. "I will not apologise for doing exemplary work to find out who killed Arthur. Your substantial ego can handle a woman conducting an investigation. Many women are just as capable as men."

"I hasten to agree." Emma Wainwright stood in the doorway. "And I'd go as far as to say most women are more capable than many men realise. Some are even better than men. Don't you agree, Miss Vale?"

Chapter 19

Emma strode into the room dressed in a practical tweed skirt and a matching jacket, her small fluffy dog tucked under one arm. Her stern gaze was fixed on me, awaiting my answer.

"I couldn't agree more," I said. "Men have long underestimated us. It was a pity it took a world war to reveal our capabilities to them."

"I've always been aware of women's abilities," Inspector Templeton said. "Good morning, Mrs Wainwright."

"I had to intervene when I heard the nature of your conversation," Emma said. "Women's role in society has always fascinated me. I've written about it a time or two, although most editors were reluctant to print my articles. They considered them unseemly."

"If you're still interested in writing, I could put in a word for you at the London Times. Although, it's not always a female-friendly place," I said.

"I have little spare time, but perhaps in the future," Emma said.

Alice had been watching our conversation in silence. She collected the tea tray she'd brought in with her, gave us a brief nod, and scuttled out. I understood Emma would intimidate most people, but I appreciated her being a champion of fairness to an underserved group in society.

"Are you here to update me about my brother's murder?" Emma addressed the question to Inspector Templeton.

"There's no new information. We still have a prime suspect, but we need additional evidence before securing a conviction," he said.

"I am terribly sorry for your loss," I said. "I enjoyed Arthur's company."

"My brother was a nincompoop." Emma adjusted her dog's collar and sighed. "But he was family, so I shall miss him. I'm glad to have seen you, Miss Vale. I understand from a conversation with Lady Sybil that you're writing Arthur's obituary."

I nodded. "I hope to. I've yet to receive an official instruction from the family, though."

"You have it from me, but I don't want her ladyship to interfere." Emma spoke the last three words with a note of derision souring the tone. "And keep the obituary short. There's no need to spend unnecessary money. I intend for the funeral to be basic. There'll be no expensive flowers or a handcrafted coffin. Despite what Lady Sybil is attempting to arrange, Arthur wasn't her husband, and I'm in charge of the funeral, since I was his closest family."

"Oh! Of course," I said. "Your parents?"

"No longer with us. There are few of us left. Just an elderly aunt I visit from time to time," Emma said. "My parents were practically minded, too. They left me their modest home, which I may stay in until I marry again."

My ears pricked. I hadn't seriously considered Emma a suspect until that point, but perhaps Arthur had been pressuring Emma to marry again, and she wanted her situation to remain the same. Could she have done something as drastic as killing Arthur to ensure her life didn't change?

"What will you do with the house now?" Inspector Templeton must have been considering the same possibility, given his question.

Emma's smile was benign. "If that's your discreet way of asking when I'm marrying again, I am in no uncertain terms a confirmed widow. And I see this face in the mirror every day, so I'm aware I'm not a bright young thing. I'm content with my simple life."

"Was Arthur happy for you to remain in the family home?" Inspector Templeton asked. "He wasn't concerned you were lonely?"

"He had no concerns about my wellbeing," Emma said. "Arthur lived here in the lap of luxury, and told me frequently how small and old-fashioned the house was. It suits my needs. I only need a small space since it's just me and the dog."

"If you don't mind me saying, you don't seem sad Arthur is gone," I said. "You weren't close?"

Emma stroked her dog's fur into place. "I'm sure you've noticed, I'm a plain speaker. And... the war hardened me. Much like Lady Sybil, I loathe war. Too much loss and devastation."

"Did you have an active role during the Great War?" I asked.

"Not overseas, but I helped with the land army," Emma said. "We all thought it was safe work. Hard and long hours, but rewarding. It felt good to do one's bit and serve the country. But there was an incident."

"What happened?" I asked.

"A German plane got into trouble and dropped its payload. A bomb landed in the field we were working in and it exploded. Several of the women were killed. It was an awful experience. After that, I hardened my heart to an excess of feeling." Emma's expression was impassive as she stared at the wall. "I focus on practicalities, rather than blubbering over things I cannot change. Just like I can't bring those innocent, hardworking women back, I can't reverse what happened to Arthur."

This wasn't the first time I'd met people grievously affected by the war, shielding their emotions for fear they'd lose control. I wasn't sure it was healthy, but people coped in different ways.

"Let me know what you want for Arthur's obituary, and I'll be happy to write it," I said.

"I appreciate that." Emma turned to the door.

"Before you go." I ignored Inspector Templeton's grumbling and muttering. If he had a mind to, he could ask the questions just as quickly as I could.

"Go ahead," Emma said. "Was there something else you needed?"

"We need details about the night of Arthur's death," I said. "I trust the police have kept you fully informed as to the situation?"

"Naturally, we have," Inspector Templeton said. "Mrs Wainwright receives daily updates."

"I do. Although it's unnecessary," Emma said. "You'll soon charge the chap you have in custody."

I decided not to tell Emma that Todd had been released. I didn't want her kicking up a stink and getting him back in handcuffs. It seemed Inspector Templeton hadn't informed Emma of this news, either, and he made no move to. Maybe we were both a touch intimidated by this practical-minded, plain-speaking woman.

"I spoke to Lady Sybil's uncle John the other day," I said. "He told me you escorted him to his bedroom on the night of the party."

"I did. Do you consider a crippled man a suspect in the murder?" Emma raised her eyebrows. "John is usually so drunk, he's barely able to get out of his chair unassisted."

"I'm aware. I took him for a spin around the village and we had a chat," I said.

"So you know of his limitations," Emma said. "Don't distract yourself with John. He spends most of the day drunk and the rest of the time asleep. He's only a threat to himself or the unfortunate folk he bashes into with his chair."

"We're covering all bases," Inspector Templeton said, helpfully backing me up.

"If you say so, but you're wasting your time," Emma said. "I always keep an eye on John when we're at the same parties. We've met numerous times since Arthur began his acquaintance with Lady Sybil. As I feared he would, John drank too much and was at risk of running over guests. And he almost smashed into an expensive vase in the hallway. When I saw him careening off and hit a wall, I decided he'd had enough fun. I grabbed his wheelchair and took him to his bedroom."

"John mentioned you put an end to his fun," I said.

Emma smirked. "I imagine he wasn't best pleased to be pushed around by a woman, but I had to set him right. He was making a fool of himself and causing trouble. I took him into his room and told him to pull himself together."

"Did he oblige?" I asked.

"I made sure he did," Emma said. "After I closed his bedroom door, I waited outside until I heard him snoring. He was so drunk, he wouldn't have stirred until the morning. But even if he did, he's not your man. How would John have gotten to the pub to attack Arthur? After that, I also retired. I'd had enough of seeing women make fools of themselves with all that dancing and champagne. It's not my sort of thing."

"Why did you come to the party if you knew you wouldn't enjoy it?"

"Arthur begged me to. He was worried I was turning into a recluse." Emma gave a horse-like snort, causing her dog to jump. "I'm not reclusive, but I prefer my own company to other people. There's no point in pretending to be something you're not."

"Quite right," I said.

"Now, I must go." Emma patted her dog's head. "Grace only had a short run first thing and gets anxious if we don't get out in the fresh air after breakfast."

"We won't detain you any longer," Inspector Templeton said.

Emma left the room, talking softly to Grace.

"You like her, don't you?" Inspector Templeton said to me.

"Emma is sensible and has strong opinions. Good opinions about women's place in society, men making fools of themselves, and she likes dogs. By my standards, she's an excellent person."

"What about the motive she served about wanting to keep the family house?" Inspector Templeton kept his voice lowered.

"I wondered about that, but Arthur was a generous sort, and as Emma said, why would he force her out of a small, dated family home when he had all this luxury?"

"Because things weren't going well with Lady Sybil. Arthur wanted to cool things off, and he needed a place to stay."

"Why not stay with Emma? There was no need to tip his sister out or force her into an unsuitable marriage so he could have the place to himself." I shook my head. "Emma's too sensible for murder."

"Where does that leave us?" Inspector Templeton asked after a second of silence.

I walked to the window and looked at the pleasant, groomed gardens. "Emma was asleep in her room. Lady Sybil was also in bed, after being assisted by her maid, Alice. Alice herself has the fearsome Cook as her alibi, and no reason for wanting to murder Arthur."

Inspector Templeton joined me by the window. "And Peter and John were too drunk or incapable of committing murder. I ask again. Who do we have left?"

"No one!" I knew exactly what he wanted me to say, but I refused to entertain the words in my mouth.

Inspector Templeton surprised me by resting a hand briefly on my shoulder. "When someone you know is involved in a terrible crime, it's hard to accept. You look at all other options, rather than the sad option, the only option, staring you in the face."

I stepped away from him, my temper firing. "How many members of your family or close friends have been involved in murder?"

"Don't be obtuse, Veronica. We've looked at all the suspects, and we keep coming back to the same person."

"Todd Smythe isn't a killer."

"We've ruled out everybody else!"

I wouldn't accept it. I couldn't. I'd missed a clue, or a suspect. Whatever it took, I'd find who actually murdered Arthur.

Chapter 20

I'd invited Ruby to meet me at her favourite restaurant, the Savoy Supper Club, after work the next day. I'd had a busy time in the office, writing obituaries to meet the printer's deadline, but the ongoing murder investigation had troubled my thoughts. I never like to admit Inspector Templeton was right. I had to keep digging into what happened at Lady Sybil's party and then afterwards at the Drunken Duck. There was a gap in my knowledge, but I'd yet to find a source to suitably fill it.

I sipped on my gin fizz and checked the time. As usual, Ruby was fifteen minutes late. She'd been summoned back to work by Lady M, and since Todd had been discharged from the hospital, she'd gone in for an hour. Knowing Lady M, that hour would have turned into five, as she'd issued various demands Ruby would have been at pains to fulfil.

The restaurant door opened, and Ruby hurried in, looking flustered and pretty in a smart patterned work dress with a dropped waistline that stopped at her knees. A waiter brought her to the table, and she settled in with a sigh. Ruby took a large sip from the dry martini I'd bought for her and sank back in her seat.

"Has Lady M been misbehaving again?" I asked, after giving her a moment to relax.

"Just being her usual horror," Ruby said. "I'm glad you arranged this evening. All I've had is stress and worry since this dreadful business with Arthur flared up."

"That's what I wanted to talk to you about." I'd decided to break the bad news to Ruby over a delicious meal and drinks to soften the blow.

Ruby sipped more martini. "I'm excited to hear about your progress on the case. Have you uncovered something new? No, wait. It was Inspector Templeton, wasn't it? He's found Todd's attacker? Please say he has and my worries will vanish. The attacker confessed to hitting you and Todd and ending Arthur's life."

"Not quite."

"Is some of that true?"

"Not yet."

Ruby flapped her linen napkin at me before settling it into her lap. "Veronica! Don't hold out on me. What do you know?"

There was no easy way to say this. "The police have gotten no further with the investigation."

Ruby peered at the menu, but she always ordered the same thing when we came here. She adored the beef stroganoff. "Then it was you who found a new suspect? You always run rings around the police. They should put you in charge of the entire Metropolitan Police. That would sort them out."

"And raise a few eyebrows!"

"I should say."

I'd briefly updated Ruby on the telephone about the visit to Lady Sybil's, but she didn't know all the details, so I spent ten minutes filling her in. By the time I was done, we'd ordered our food and almost finished our first round of drinks.

"How frustrating. Where does this leave Todd?" Ruby asked.

"In a pickle," I said. "I attempted to dissuade Inspector Templeton from seeing Todd as the prime suspect, but he won't budge. We went round in circles discussing other suspects, but he kept drawing me back to the same unsatisfying conclusion."

"That my brother is a cold-hearted killer?" Ruby shook her head. "I refuse to believe it. Todd is many things, but he's not cruel or unkind. Even when we were growing up, he was a sweetie. He could be irritating though, and he went through a dreadful phase of hiding worms in my shoes just to make me squeal."

"I'll keep trying with Inspector Templeton, but I fear he has a single-minded focus on Todd. He's looking for evidence or a confession. Don't be surprised if you get a telephone call from Todd to say he's back at the police station."

Ruby grabbed my hand. "We should send him away before they make an arrest. He could go to America. There are opportunities over there. And they'd adore his accent."

"If Todd goes anywhere other than the local pub, home, or to visit you, he'll look guilty," I said. "Only an innocent man would stay to see this through to the end."

"What if the end is Inspector Templeton's version? He could take this case to court with Todd as the only suspect." Ruby blinked away tears.

"I don't think he's foolish enough to go that far. At least not yet," I said. "But with Lady Sybil keeping a close eye on things and the ever-practical Emma in the wings, he won't want to keep this case open for much longer."

"If we can't get Todd out of the country, I don't know what we should do," Ruby said. "Prepare for the worst, but hope for the best?"

"It's good to keep positive thoughts front and centre. I'm not giving up, and neither should you."

Our food arrived. Ruby's beef stroganoff looked delicious, and I'd opted for a hearty plate of shepherd's pie with mashed potato topping.

"I'm not sure I can eat," Ruby said, then spent several minutes filling her face and making noises of contentment.

I was happy to let her eat and ruminate. Delicious food was comforting in times of crisis, and I'd deliberately picked the supper club because they made the best martinis, and their dessert cart was the stuff of dreams. If I couldn't bring Ruby good news, I would fill her with wonderful food to cheer her up.

When Ruby came up for air, her plate half empty, I set down my fork. "I can draw only one conclusion. A suspect has been lying to all of us."

"Yes!" Ruby nodded with vigour. "But which one?"

"Lady Sybil concealed the fiery nature of her relationship with Arthur," I said. "But she was eventually open about the reality of their situation. And if she killed

Arthur, she'd lose everything. She values her freedom. I got the impression she had a miserable marriage."

"She wouldn't want to swap one cage for another," Ruby said. "And Lady Sybil has a decent alibi. The maid saw her to bed."

"Arthur's sister, Emma, is also practical. We winkled out a possible motive for her wanting Arthur out of the picture, but she stayed at the mansion that night. And Alice checked the guest rooms before she went to bed herself. No one was missing."

"From the sounds of it, Peter and John were too drunk to tie their own shoelaces, let alone hike along country lanes and kill a man," Ruby said glumly. "And with John in his wheelchair, it can't have been him."

"The killer was someone stealthy, with a clear head. Someone who was able to sneak into the Drunken Duck without Bridget or Arthur hearing."

"Are you sure we didn't miss anybody? Or overlook a motive?" Ruby finished the last mouthful of her stroganoff. "An old enemy from the war, perhaps?"

"Just like Todd, Arthur had a medical condition that excluded him from the front lines. I remember them discussing it at Lady Sybil's party."

"Of course. He used to get wheezy when we dashed from one party to the other. That was before he so rudely dismissed me. What about a colleague?" Ruby asked. "Someone who didn't like Arthur's way of doing things."

"He didn't introduce us to anyone at the party he worked with," I said.

"A jealous rival for Lady Sybil's affection? Many men would like to be in Arthur's position. Dating a wealthy, refined widow, with easy access to funds, and a glorious house she opens for parties."

"From all accounts, Arthur was about to step away from that relationship. Any suitor would simply have needed to bide their time, not stoop to murder."

"Maybe they didn't know things were going wrong between Lady Sybil and Arthur," Ruby said. "Jealousy makes people do terrible things."

We fell silent as our plates were cleared, drinks refilled, and the waiter returned with the dessert cart. We were temporarily distracted by thoughts of murder as a glorious array of puddings, cakes, and trifles were showcased. I selected an Eton mess with a raspberry coulis, and Ruby had a large slice of chocolate cake with cream.

"Here's an option." Ruby brandished her spoon. "Arthur's death was an accident, and the police have gotten things wrong."

Top of Form

"He died in his sleep?"

"Isn't that possible? With his weak chest, he could have taken sick in the night."

"Inspector Templeton confirmed Arthur was suffocated," I said. "And I doubt the autopsy was mishandled."

"I'm willing to believe anything at this moment. I'd rather there was a mistake than my brother go down for murder." She ate two large mouthfuls of chocolate cake, one after the other, barely pausing to chew.

"We'll keep looking for answers," I said. "I'm not giving up on Todd."

"Neither am I, even though he is the biggest ninny around. I haven't told you, but he teased me mercilessly when I talked to the handsome Doctor Knight. He said I kept blushing and giggling like a schoolgirl. As if I'd do such a thing."

"I can't imagine you would." I smiled at her. Ruby always got tongue-tied around a handsome face. "Did you get the good doctor's telephone number?"

"No, dating a doctor is a romantic notion, but they work dreadfully long hours. I want my man to be hopelessly devoted to me, not to the sick women he's looking after."

"It's probably for the best," I said. "The right one is out there for you somewhere."

"He won't want anything to do with me if I have a brother in prison," Ruby said.

"That's the spirit. How's the cake?"

Ruby pushed away her almost empty plate. "I'm too worried to eat another morsel."

"Considering your lack of hunger, you did an excellent job. I'll get the bill."

Half an hour later, and after dropping Ruby off at her small London flat, I returned home in a taxi and was warmly greeted by Benji. He'd spent the evening entertaining my mother and Pippin, since the supper club didn't allow dogs.

"Veronica! I need you. It's an emergency."

The panic in my mother's voice had me dashing along the hallway with my coat and shoes still on, my handbag clutched in a fist. I burst into her bedroom. "What is it? Are you unwell?"

"It's Pippin! She's a menace." My mother pointed under her bed. "She grabbed my slipper and snuck away. She's been chewing on it ever since. It's my favourite pair."

"Oh dear. That's unfortunate." I slumped onto the end of her bed.

"Unfortunate! It's not as if I can step out and get myself a replacement pair whenever I have a fancy for new footwear. I'll have cold feet if I have to shuffle around in my old slippers. There's a hole in the bottom of one of them."

"Don't underestimate yourself," I murmured. "When you set your mind to it, you can achieve anything."

"I didn't achieve getting the slipper out of Pippin's mouth. She's a scamp."

"We may have to put up with that adorable scamp for a while longer," I said.

"What's this?" Matthew ambled into my mother's bedroom and plonked himself beside me.

"I was about to update Mother on Todd's situation," I said. "Despite exploring every avenue, Inspector Templeton keeps returning to Todd as the killer. All the other suspects have alibis or lack the ability to kill. The police are closing in, and I'm running out of time and avenues to ensure that doesn't happen."

"Would you like me to speak to your inspector and explain what a sweet young man Todd is?" my mother asked with complete sincerity.

"If you think it will help, I'm willing to try anything," I said. "I bent Inspector Templeton's ear the whole way back from Lady Sybil's, trying to get him to see sense and keep an open mind, but he's fixed on Todd. It's most frustrating. Perhaps I should take the case to his superior."

"If you do, Inspector Templeton will never speak to you again," my mother said. "Don't worry. He'll do the right thing."

"He won't, while he's convinced the best thing to do is charge Todd with murder," I said.

"It's really that grim?" Matthew asked.

"I see no good outcome at the moment." I lay on my back and stared at the ceiling. "I need to go back to the beginning. I've missed something. I haven't yet uncovered the reason why someone wanted Arthur dead. I went over all the scenarios with Ruby this evening, but we drew blanks."

"Sleep on it," my mother said. "You must still be suffering because of your severe head injury."

"My very mild head injury is healing well," I said. "The bruise will be gone in a few days."

"You'll have a new scar, though. How many does that make?"

"Not enough to concern yourself with." I slid off the bed and peered underneath it. Pippin had a slipper firmly wedged in her mouth. She beat her tail on the floor when she saw me and wiggled her behind. I rifled through my handbag, found several dog treats, and enticed her out, returning the soggy slipper to my mother.

She inspected it with a sharp eye. "There's a hole in this one now, too. I'll get chilblains if I'm not careful. Then they'll turn into ulcers, and I'll be done for. Next thing you know, I'll be having a leg lopped off and you'll have to carry me around everywhere. That's if gangrene doesn't set in."

"We can't have that. Matthew's back won't take lumping you around. I'll buy you a new pair of slippers tomorrow," I said, still on my knees, as I petted both dogs. "Or perhaps Matthew would enjoy a trip to the shops. It's supposed to be nice weather."

He frowned. "I'm looking after the kittens."

"You could leave them for an hour to hop on a bus and buy new slippers. You don't want Mother to get chilblains that will turn into ulcers and finish her off, do you?"

He muttered to himself, but didn't agree or disagree. He was becoming almost as much of a shut-in as our mother was.

"She is a good girl, really." Mother looked on affectionately at Pippin. "She's kept me company all day when I've been left alone for hours."

"I check on you every hour!" Matthew said.

"Do you? My mind is not what it once was. What with worrying about you two, losing my precious slippers, and my concern over Todd. I've barely slept in days."

I exchanged an exasperated look with Matthew. "You have my deepest sympathy. I think I'll have an early night."

"Before you go, you need to find the rest of the bird," my mother said.

I was already on my feet and at the door when she spoke. "What bird?"

"I don't know how he did it, but Benji must have caught a bird when he was in the garden."

"He'd never do that." I looked at Benji. He didn't reveal any answers to this puzzle.

"I can't think where else the feather came from. He only let me look after much cajoling and treats, but he wouldn't let me have it. He's normally such a good boy, but he's been guarding the feather ever since you returned from Todd's lodgings after you were almost killed."

I returned to Benji and peered at him. That was out of character. "What kind of feather?"

"It was long, white, and straight. Maybe from a dove. I'm no bird fancier, though. He's probably still got it around here somewhere. You must find the rest. I don't want a bird carcass stinking up the house and bringing in the plague."

"Plague comes from rats," Matthew said cheerfully. "Or is it the fleas on rats? It's definitely not from birds."

"Then consumption. Or gout. Who knows how these things spread." Mother waved a hand as if dispersing all the illness and disease her words had conjured.

I crouched in front of Benji. "Fetch the feather, boy."

Benji lifted one paw. The feather was underneath it.

"He's had this since we came back from Todd's?" A stir of memory drifted loose as I looked at the feather. It was too large to come from a pillow.

"Oh! Perhaps. I told you he was eating something, but you wouldn't listen to me," my mother said. "He's obsessed with that feather."

I looked at the white feather, and my eyes widened. I kissed the top of Benji's head. "You clever, clever boy. You've just solved this murder."

Chapter 21

"Why must I be the one to search through the rubbish?" Ruby sounded groggy and grumpy because I'd dragged her from sleep with an early telephone call. If there was one thing Ruby adored more than cake, it was sleep.

"I need to go to the library archive." I stood in the hallway, clutching the telephone, my gaze on family photographs hung on the wall. "We must gather the final pieces of evidence to ensure Todd's innocence."

"I'm made for high society, not searching bags of rubbish like some of those poor homeless chaps we met in the park in the hopes someone threw out a bottle of gin. Why can't I go to the library?"

"Because they know me, and I have a card that gives me access to the old records. I'll send Benji over in a taxi, and he'll go through the rubbish with you. He has an excellent nose. Bridget has laid out the bags in the passageway behind the Drunken Duck, and she said you can borrow a pair of overalls and some rubber gloves."

Ruby grumbled and tutted. "Since it's my irritating brother's freedom at stake, I'll make the sacrifice."

"As soon as you find what we need, head to Lady Sybil's mansion. I've already contacted Inspector Templeton, and he's arranging for us all to be there."

"The suspects, too?"

"Precisely. But I must get to the library as soon as possible. If I'm right about this, I'll find the final nail to slam into the killer's coffin."

"I'll wait for Benji, then drive us to the Drunken Duck," Ruby said.

We said goodbye, and I set down the telephone.

"Veronica! What are you doing up so early?" My mother's voice drifted out of her bedroom.

I hurried in and greeted her. "I know who killed Arthur and made an attempt on Todd's life. But I must dash. I have evidence to gather and suspects to meet."

Her bottom lip quivered. "That sounds dangerous."

"I'm not doing this alone. Inspector Templeton is involved."

"Good. He'll protect you. Take an umbrella! The forecast is for rain today."

I was already hurrying to the door with Benji, and mumbled what I hoped my mother would think was an agreement.

"Don't ignore me! Your constitution has been weakened because of your serious head injury. If you get soaked through, the rain will finish you off."

"I'll be perfectly safe. From killers and lethal drops of rain!"

"Wait! You haven't told me who the killer is," my mother called out.

"I promise I'll reveal everything later. But I must go." I hurried outside with Benji into a most pleasant morning.

I secured a reliable, sensible cabbie who promised he'd take Benji to Ruby, and then I was in another taxi, going in the opposite direction, to the impressive newspaper archive in Colindale, north London. The British Library had established this facility to house copies of all publications, and I was a regular visitor to the dark brick building with its white stone entrance frame leading to double wooden doors.

They were just opening those doors as I approached. I presented my card and made my way to a familiar section of the library. Newspapers were carefully catalogued by year and month, so it wasn't difficult to find all articles published in April nineteen sixteen.

It took an hour of searching, but I found what I was looking for. My heart sank. What a disappointment. But I had what I needed, so I made a note of the details and dashed out, heading to busier streets, and grabbing another taxi. I offered the cabbie a bonus if he put his foot down, so I got to Lady Sybil's as soon as possible.

I wanted to telephone the Drunken Duck and see how Benji and Ruby were getting on, but I had no time to delay. When the killer realised the game was up, they might abscond.

My taxi pulled up outside Lady Sybil's mansion. There were several cars already parked, and I recognised Inspector Templeton's vehicle. I was glad he'd taken my earlier telephone call seriously, although he hadn't been happy with how elusive I'd been. But I'd assured him I knew who killed Arthur and how I'd prove it.

Ruby stood outside the front door with Benji beside her. He bounded over, happy to see me when I climbed out of the taxi after paying the driver.

I gave Benji a pat on the head and strode over to join Ruby. She wore a sour expression and still had on the oversized overall Bridget had kindly loaned her.

"Did you get what we needed?" I asked.

"I did. Safely secured and with Inspector Templeton. But I fell over twice while searching in the muck and landed in something most unpleasant. I bruised my right buttock."

"Your bruised buttock can join my bruised hip, and they can sympathise together," I said. "I got what I needed too. Is everybody inside?"

"They are." Inspector Templeton appeared in the doorway. "And before you take another step, I need to know exactly what you have planned."

"You must trust me by now, Inspector," I said. "Have I ever let you down?"

He sighed. "Lady Sybil is unhappy. She's talking about contacting my superior."

"Then let's give her every reason to be happy by solving this murder," I said. "What are we waiting for?"

"You! We've been waiting for you," Ruby said. "I didn't think I'd have time to get changed, so I left my dress at the Drunken Duck. Will people think less of me looking like this?"

"You're a hard-working, enterprising woman with a good head on her shoulders. If anyone thinks less of you because of your clothing, they're not worth knowing," I said as we strode into the house. "Let's clear your brother's name, shall we?"

Ruby nodded and tucked her hand into my elbow as we walked behind Inspector Templeton and into the sitting room, Benji stuck in between us. Lady Sybil was there, along with Peter, John, Emma, and Todd.

"Miss Vale, you know how to make an entrance," Lady Sybil said, from her seat by the window. "This is all very dramatic. Telephone calls demanding a visit, and everyone assembling with little idea as to what is going on."

"It's not my intention to dazzle or show off," I said. "And I appreciate everyone attending at such short notice."

"I can't understand why you're still involved," Lady Sybil said. "Inspector Templeton confirmed you aren't an active member of the police, but everywhere I look, there you are."

"That is true. But we make a good team, and we always find ourselves working together. One might say Inspector Templeton and I are a match made in heaven. Isn't that right, Inspector?"

He appeared too stunned to respond.

I smiled at his shocked expression, then grew serious. "I won't keep you long. I'm sure you all want to find out what happened to Arthur."

We remained standing. Ruby to my left, Inspector Templeton to my right, and Benji by my feet.

"I thought this chap was to be charged with my brother's murder." Emma pointed to Todd.

Todd ducked his head and tucked his hands in his trouser pockets. "I promise, it wasn't me."

"Things looked bleak for Todd for a time. He had a fight with Arthur on the night of his death, and he hid that he'd requested money from Arthur when the police questioned him," I said.

"I also heard he had no alibi." John wheeled closer, his hip flask resting on his thigh.

"Several charming homeless men confirmed Todd was in the local park," I said. "And when he woke, he stumbled off in the opposite direction to the Drunken Duck. Todd is innocent."

"If it wasn't him, are you saying it was one of us?" Peter looked askance.

"Your name has been mentioned as a suspect, but when we spoke at the hospital, you were genuinely sad about losing your friend," I said. "Other than disagreeing with each other during a game of billiards, we could find no substantial motive for you wanting Arthur dead."

"And Lady Sybil's maid, Alice, supplied us with a solid alibi for you," Inspector Templeton said.

I looked around. "Of course! Alice must be here, too."

"Why must my maid be in attendance?" Lady Sybil enquired. "Is she the killer?"

"Alice has knowledge that will reveal who is. Would you summon her, Lady Sybil?"

Not looking amused at being ordered around, Lady Sybil rang for her butler, who delivered a trembling Alice into the room a few moments later.

"Have I done something wrong?" Alice asked, not sure who she should address the question to.

"Not as far as I'm aware," Lady Sybil said. "Miss Vale insisted you be here, and we're all excited to hear her logic."

"You've done nothing wrong," I said to Alice. "You're innocent of any criminal wrongdoing."

"Blimey! I didn't realise anyone considered me a criminal." Alice's eyes were wide.

"You were briefly on the suspect list. But Inspector Templeton spoke with your gentleman friend this morning, and he confirmed you're devoted to each other. You have no motive for wanting Arthur dead."

Inspector Templeton nodded. "I had a conversation with the butcher's apprentice. He comes from a respectable family."

"He said he's devoted to me?" Alice's cheeks glowed, and she smiled.

"You have nothing to worry about, Alice," I said. "But please, stay."

She nodded, her smile fading and her eyes remaining wide with concern.

"Lady Sybil, if I may turn to you next," I said.

"Inspector, I admire you for working with a woman, but if you're intending to let Miss Vale point the finger of blame at me, we shall have a problem," Lady Sybil said.

Inspector Templeton tensed. "Miss Vale's character is excellent. She also has a keen eye and an inquisitive mind. I wish more of my officers were like her. I'm comfortable allowing her sensible judgement to uncover the truth about Arthur's murder."

If I hadn't been so focused on outlining clues and suspects, I would have flushed from my toes to my hairline. I would have to remember to thank him for those compliments.

"It's rare you find a man who talks like that about a woman," Emma said. "Well done, Inspector."

"I couldn't agree more," I said. "Lady Sybil, you were a suspect because you concealed the serious nature of your argument with Arthur and exaggerated his fondness for you."

"And my motive?"

"Arthur lost interest in your relationship, but you didn't want to let him go."

"I hope that after our conversations, you changed your opinion of me," Lady Sybil said.

"I was initially surprised when you requested an advertisement in the London Times to find a new partner so soon after Arthur's death. It seemed immensely practical. One might say, cold-hearted."

"I make no apologies for being practical or for making that request," Lady Sybil said. "I'll find a new man to step out with by whatever means necessary. I refuse to be lonely. And I refuse to be unhappy. I am sad Arthur is gone, but we had a sensible arrangement."

"Yet you attempted to fool me by saying Arthur was utterly devoted to you and had no interest in your money," I said.

Lady Sybil settled her hands into her lap and lifted her chin. "I may be practical, but I also have dreams. The early part of my life was miserable. My family was repressed, my husband a dreary sort with no sense of humour, and I wondered if my life would comprise grey obligations. Then I was free. My parents are dead, my husband is gone. I saw an opportunity for joy. I will not let that go."

"Good for you," Ruby said. "We all deserve joy. Perhaps I should place an advertisement for a suitable chap. My current methods have only led me to cads and cheats."

"We'll discuss that another time," I murmured.

Ruby's eyes gleamed with amusement, and I could imagine her mentally creating her advertisement.

"Although we considered you a suspect," I said to Lady Sybil, "you value your freedom too highly to do something as reckless as murder. And Alice assured us you were settled in your room for the night."

"Correct. I wouldn't creep along a country lane, sneak into a pub, and smother my lover. That would be distasteful." Lady Sybil's stern expression softened. "And you're right. I highly prize my freedom."

I looked at Inspector Templeton. "Where is the evidence Ruby found?"

"You have evidence to prove who killed Arthur?" Peter asked. "What is it?"

Inspector Templeton opened his jacket and pulled a small bag from his pocket, which he placed on the coffee table in the middle of the neatly arranged seating. There was a long white feather inside the bag. I extracted the feather Benji had smartly secured and placed them side by side. They were almost identical.

Everyone stared at the feathers.

"Are they supposed to have some meaning?" Lady Sybil asked.

"Only to the killer," I said. "And on their own, they mean nothing. The first feather, which was left in Arthur's room at the Drunken Duck pub, was misplaced when he struggled and tore a pillow. If it weren't for my dog and my determined best friend, who never give up when presented with a challenge, that feather would have been lost forever."

Benji wagged his tail, while Ruby smoothed a hand down the front of her fetching overalls.

"I'm the one who's lost," Peter said. "What have feathers got to do with murder?"

I lifted a finger. "Todd was attacked at his home. I believe his attacker was the same person who murdered Arthur. And for the same reason. They left an almost identical feather in Todd's lodgings."

"The same killer?" Peter was shaking his head. "I know both chaps well. I can't imagine anyone would want to harm them."

"It wasn't until I found the feathers that everything clicked into place." I looked at Emma, who had gone silent, her hands clenched by her sides as she glared at the feathers. "Then I remembered Emma told me she wrote articles for the local press. So, first thing this morning, I went to the newspaper archives. The articles I perused revealed the reason Emma murdered Arthur."

Chapter 22

The group gawped at Emma, who remained resolutely silent, staring at me.

"Why would Emma murder her brother?" John asked.

"Do you want to tell everyone about the content of your articles?" I asked Emma.

"That was a long time ago," Emma said. "And I couldn't have killed Arthur. I was here."

"Alone in your room," I said. "And you were specific when I spoke to you. You said you took John to his bedroom, left him there, and went to bed. You didn't have to supply me with that information. I didn't ask for it. Yet you felt the need to tell me, to make sure you didn't look guilty."

"Will someone tell me what the articles said?" Lady Sybil asked.

"Emma was vocal about her dislike of war, but her articles told a different story. She believes all men should have served," I said. "She was a member of the Order of the White Feather, a group of campaigners who would accost men and present them with white feathers. Those feathers symbolised their cowardice for not signing up."

There were several gasps.

"I suspect, when Emma overheard Arthur and Todd joking about how lucky they were to be unhealthy enough to avoid getting called up, it triggered something in her, and she acted. Arthur was family, but he'd done wrong in her eyes and needed to pay," I explained.

"Emma would never kill her brother," Lady Sybil said. "This makes no sense."

"It didn't to me, not until I read the articles. Perhaps Emma made allowances for Arthur because they were related, but when she heard him making a joke of avoiding serving, it was too much."

Emma continued her silence.

Inspector Templeton cleared his throat, as if he was about to intervene, but I beat him to it. I knew what I'd presented so far wouldn't be enough to secure a conviction.

"I don't think Emma would have acted if she hadn't been encouraged. John, you complained about Emma when she forced you to leave the party, but the way you spoke about her suggests you know each other well," I said.

He lifted a shoulder. "I wouldn't say that. Our paths have crossed ever since Arthur and Lady Sybil got involved, so we've met a handful of times."

"I also remembered you saying how useless you were and how you wished you'd been able to fight. You even said it was every man's duty to do his bit. Every woman, too."

"I stand by that," John said. "I want to be useful, but I can't be in this chair."

"I suspect you had similar conversations with Emma. You may even have recognised her name from her articles, condemning men who didn't fight. The two of you, heads together, discussing the world's injustice, must have impassioned her into action. You even mentioned Emma's comment that there were some not fit to serve, so you discussed the war."

"Hold on a moment. Are you attempting to implicate me in Arthur's murder, too?" John shook his head. "I'm stuck in this chair!"

"You are. However, as I assured you, you're still very capable."

"I'm not sure where you're going with this," Inspector Templeton muttered to me.

I turned to Alice. "You're concerned there are mice in the house, aren't you?"

She shot a worried look at Lady Sybil. "I have been hearing an odd squeaking sound. I guessed it was mice."

"Does it sound like this?" I strode to John's chair and pushed it. The wheels had to complete a full rotation before there was a small, high-pitched squeak.

"Oh! Yes. That's the sound," Alice said.

"And you heard that noise after the party ended, didn't you?"

"Unhand my chair, woman!" John grabbed the wheels and pushed himself away from me.

Alice nodded. "Yes. We ... we don't have mice?"

"You most likely do. Most country estates have mice," I said. "My point is, Alice heard Emma assisting John in his chair the night Arthur died. They went to the Drunken Duck, most likely in a car. John acted as Emma's lookout while she snuck inside and smothered Arthur. She'd planned on leaving a coward's feather on his body, but in the chaos with the ripped pillow, the feather got lost."

There were several seconds of stunned silence.

"Did Emma also attack me?" Todd asked.

"She's the right height, and isn't muscular," I said. "Emma wasn't content to end Arthur's life. You needed to be gone, too. You were both marked as cowards and had no value in society."

"How very dare you," Ruby said. "I'm the only one allowed to attack my darling ninny of a brother."

"You can't prove any of this," Emma said. "A few radical articles, a squeaking chair, and feathers mean nothing."

It was a frustratingly fair point, but when there were two criminals, it was an easier task to get one of them to talk.

"Perhaps whoever is most cooperative will be looked upon leniently by the police. Don't you agree, Inspector Templeton?" I asked.

"A reduced sentence would be an option if we receive key information from one of you," he said.

Emma and John stared at each other. No one spoke. Benji gave a gentle whine.

Emma drew in a breath.

"It was her! She's lost her marbles. I had nothing to do with this. I'm leaving." John wheeled his chair to the door, but Emma beat him to it, shoving him out of the way with a harsh kick that sent him flying across the wooden floor, until his wheels snagged on the rug.

"I've heard enough." Inspector Templeton marched over and prevented Emma from leaving. "You're both under arrest for murder."

I was enjoying a cheese and tomato sandwich at Arthur's wake, held in the dining room at Lady Sybil's home, when Ruby hurried over with Todd and Peter in tow. Ten days had passed since Emma and John had been charged with Arthur's murder, and Arthur's aunt had been kind enough to extend an invitation to all of us to attend his wake and say a final goodbye.

"Arthur would have been happy with how many people turned out to see him off," Peter said.

"It was a much more acceptable service than Emma had planned." Lady Sybil appeared, dressed in somber black, with a lace veil over her face. She nodded at me. "Thank you, Miss Vale. I appreciate your hard work and tenacity. I'll be in touch regarding my advertisement."

"You're most welcome," I said as she turned away. "I shall look forward to hearing from you."

"Peter thinks we should go dancing after the wake," Ruby said once Lady Sybil had left. "He said it was what Arthur would have wanted."

Peter looked startled. "It was only a suggestion, not an invitation. I... I'll be back soon." He dashed away after Lady Sybil.

"I think he's ever so handsome," Ruby said.

"Peter? You'd decided he wasn't of good character," I said. "Have you had a change of heart?"

"He's been thoroughly decent recently. I made a mistake with him. I'm giving him a second chance."

"You haven't made any mistakes," Todd said. "Peter's immense fun, but he's financially worse off than me. He has a good job, but a problem with the cards. He needs a lady with money, old bean, and you have little of that. I suppose you could sell the Ghost. Then you can wine and dine Peter to keep him interested."

Ruby pursed her lips as she glared at Peter's back. "Never! She was a precious gift, and she drives like a dream."

"She was a gift from a man old enough to be your father who had less than pure intentions towards you," Todd said.

"His intentions were grey around the edges, but I held my own," Ruby said. "And the car was compensation for his poor behaviour towards me. I'll never give up my darling Ghost."

"You should get a bicycle." Todd chuckled. "That'll keep you fit."

"I'm as fit as a flea. Fitter than you, anyway." Ruby jabbed a finger into Todd's ribs.

"We should be grateful for Todd's poor health," I said. "If it weren't for Emma coming after him because of his heart condition, we would never have figured out that Emma and John killed Arthur."

"It was jolly clever of you to puzzle through the clues," Todd said. "I never thought a woman would attack me, though. I'm humiliated."

"As I'm always telling you, we're very capable," Ruby said. "We can turn our hand to anything—murder, fixing cars, solving crimes, dealing with ninny-headed brothers who won't take life seriously."

As they bickered as only brother and sister could, I spotted Inspector Templeton on the other side of the room. I walked over to him with Benji and waited until he'd finished speaking to another mourner before joining him.

"The service had a good turnout," I said.

"Arthur was well liked." Inspector Templeton wore a black suit with a smart white shirt underneath. His shoes were polished to a high shine.

"Any updates you'd like to share with me?" I inspected my plate of food.

He almost smiled. "I'm surprised you've stayed away this long before asking. You must have been itching to grill me during the eulogies."

"Inspector! I have some decorum."

This time, he did chuckle. "I spoke to John again this morning. He confessed he had got in over his head. He got drunk one evening and spoke to Emma about his beliefs. Then she wouldn't leave him alone. She became obsessed and wanted to take action against the cowards who humiliated this country during the Great War. He claims he never thought she was serious."

"But he's still admitting he was an accomplice in Arthur's murder?"

"He is. Although he said he only went along to talk Emma out of killing Arthur." Inspector Templeton's gaze moved around the crowd. "I'm not so sure. We've been looking into his background some more and there are old connections with black market trading. There's nothing honest about that man."

"I'm glad Todd is free and I could reunite him with Pippin." I looked around the dining room and discovered Pippin begging for food from a bemused-looking elderly lady, wearing a black hat with long feathers bobbing about on the top.

"I also had a long conversation with Emma's aunt," Inspector Templeton said.

"That poor woman. She's lost two relatives because of this dreadful business."

"She was deeply concerned about Emma's state of mind," Inspector Templeton said. "She's been trying to get her to see a doctor because she was worried about her obsession with the war."

"Emma was unhinged?"

"According to her aunt, she hasn't been right since her husband died," Inspector Templeton said. "She obsessed over the men who didn't serve and couldn't get past that. Her actions could have been her way of coping with the grief."

"The things people hide behind sensible facades," I murmured. "When I spoke to Emma, I would never have known she had so much torment inside her."

"The things people hide from the public in general would shock you."

"I'm extremely hard to shock."

"I'm convinced of that! Emma is a troubled lady. She is undergoing an assessment, but I believe she'll be fit to stand trial," Inspector Templeton said.

"And Arthur will get the justice he deserves."

We sipped our drinks and stood together in a pleasingly comfortable silence, the hum of mourners' gossip drifting around us in the opulent room.

"Arthur's aunt expressed an interest in setting up a lasting memorial for her nephew," Inspector Templeton said. "I know you have a memorial wall at the dogs' home. I mentioned it to her, and she was very interested."

"That would be fitting," I said. "It would be nice to see Arthur's name immortalised in such a warm, loving place."

Ruby dashed over, mischief shining in her eyes as she waggled her eyebrows. "I hope I'm not interrupting anything."

"We were talking about the case." I speared her with a glare, as a warning to behave.

"If you'll excuse me," Inspector Templeton said. "I have loose ends to tie up at work."

We said our goodbyes, and I watched him go.

"Was Inspector Templeton asking you on a date?" Ruby pinched a sandwich from my plate.

"No! And he never will. We're ... business partners. Even though he doesn't like to admit it, I'm his hidden asset."

"He did admit it. He very much admitted it in front of everyone in Lady Sybil's sitting room," Ruby said. "I was stunned."

"Oh! Yes, I've yet to thank him for those kind words." I searched through the crowd of mourners, but Inspector Templeton had disappeared. He was a good man. He recognised my abilities, and he wasn't afraid to work with them. Well, not always afraid. Timid at most.

Benji walked over and sat between us, looking happy, no doubt his stomach full of finger sandwiches and cake he wasn't supposed to have.

Ruby looked around the room and sighed. "There's no one here."

"Are you seeking someone in particular?" I asked.

"A suitable man! I know it's not the most appropriate place, but I thought some of Arthur's friends may be appealing. Nobody has caught my eye. Or if they have, there's a sharp-eyed woman with them. Where are all the good men?"

"You need a dog," I said. "Dogs are so loyal."

"I'm not ready to become an animal-mad spinster just yet."

"I am," I said with a laugh. "It's the best way to be."

Inspector Templeton reappeared and strode towards me. "Veronica, there's someone outside asking for you. They're driving a Harrod's van."

"That's someone from the dogs' home. I wasn't expecting anyone to pick me up." I hurried outside with Ruby, Benji, and Inspector Templeton. A large American-built Walker van had been donated to the charity by the department store Harrods, and was regularly used for shorter journeys, since batteries powered it.

Molly poked her head out of the driver's window. "I tried you at your house, but your mother said you were here. I hope you don't mind me showing up."

"What's wrong?" I hurried over to join her with the others.

"We found an enormous puppy farm. We need all hands on deck to clear them as quickly as possible."

I looked at Ruby. "Are you sure you don't want a dog? Puppies are cute, and we won't have room for all of them at the dogs' home."

"I should say not," Molly said. "We'll need at least a dozen foster homes."

"You always have mine. Matthew will be happy to take on some puppies," I said. "Ruby?"

She rolled her eyes. "I'll help, but I have no space for puppies. Adorable furry babies with teeth would ruin my clothes and shred my upholstery."

We hurried around the side of the van, and Benji and Ruby hopped inside to be greeted by several more volunteers.

I looked back at Inspector Templeton. "Well, Jacob? Are you helping to save the day?"

He smiled as he took off his jacket and rolled up his sleeves. "The paperwork can wait. Let's go see about those puppies."

Historical notes

My research for Death at the Drunken Duck took me along some fascinating avenues I want to share with readers. Let's start with the dogs!

Dog shows

In the United Kingdom, dog shows began in the early 19th century, often hosted at agricultural and sporting exhibitions, where working breeds were shown off for their abilities in herding, hunting, and guarding.

Things became more formal in 1859 with a show in Newcastle-on-Tyne, England. It was created by Mr. Thomas Pearce, who was a sportsman and dog fan.

The Kennel Club was created in 1873 and led on dog shows, creating breed standards and a registry for pedigrees. Dog shows swiftly gained popularity across the world and included dogs' performance and their appearance.

I based the charity dog show on an informal model, with fun events for agility and ball chase, and with no judgement over any dog's appearance or breed. After all, the only thing that matters with a dog is that he's healthy and happy.

Location

Byfleet Manor was my inspiration for Montague Mansion, Lady Sybil Montague's home.

The manor is a Grade II listed house in Byfleet, Surrey, England, and has been used as a filming location in several television series, including Downton Abbey, Poirot, and Cranford.

Byfleet Manor began as a royal hunting lodge but was rebuilt around 1685 after it fell into ruin. It passed from owner to owner and wasn't well cared for until 1905, when it was restored and enlarged to its current layout.

Rather charmingly, its current owners allow public events, including 1920s-themed tea parties, which seem most appropriate for Veronica and Ruby.

The Drunken Duck pub

The joy of writing fiction is the creative license I'm given! I found a wonderful pub in the wrong part of the country. So, I picked it up and moved it to Surrey!!

The actual Drunken Duck Inn can be found in Ambleside, in the glorious Lake District. It sits at a crossroads and was once a farmhouse. The building's owners have kept a lot of its *olde worlde* charm and the inn has a cosy interior with wooden floors and dried hops hanging on the walls.

If you're ever in that area, ask to see the bedroom where the landlady discovered Arthur's body!

Also by

Death at the Fireside Inn
Death at the Drunken Duck
Death that the Craven Arms

More mysteries coming soon. While you wait, why not investigate the back catalogue of K.E. O'Connor (Kitty's alter ego.)

About the author

Immerse yourself into Kitty Kildare's cleverly woven historical British mysteries. Follow the mystery in the Veronica Vale Investigates series and enjoy the dazzle and delights of 1920s England. Kitty is a not-so-secret pen name of established cozy mystery author K.E. O'Connor, who decided she wanted to time travel rather than cast spells! Enjoy the twists and turns.

Join in the fun and get Kitty's newsletter (and secret wartime files about our sleuthing ladies!)

Newsletter: https://BookHip.com/JJPKDLB
Website: www.kittykildare.com
Facebook: www.facebook.com/kittykildare

www.ingramcontent.com/pod-product-compliance
Lightning Source LLC
Chambersburg PA
CBHW061431210726
48287CB00007B/2170